A DOOR FOR THE WORD

A DOOR FOR THE WORD

Thirty-six new hymns
2002–2005

by
TIMOTHY
DUDLEY-SMITH

Written since the collected edition,

A House of Praise

Oxford University Press

Hope Publishing Company

'. . .pray for us also, that God may open to us a door for the word, to declare the mystery of Christ. . .'

Colossians 4.3, RSV

CONTENTS

The indexes above, taken together with those in *A House of Praise,* form a complete index of subjects and first lines to all my hymn texts, up to the Spring of 2005.

T.D.S.

Foreword

One Good Friday, when I was aged about twelve, the new headmaster of my school felt that his pupils should occupy some of their free time on that special day in serious reading. He set out a number of books from his own shelves for us to choose from, few of which, if I remember rightly, seemed to promise much in the way of entertainment. So I took a small blue volume in the Oxford 'World's Classics' series, by an author apparently called Tolstoy, entitled *Twenty-three Tales*. Later I bought the same edition for myself. One of those stories, about a man called Pahóm, has a bearing on this present book, as I shall shortly show.

A little over a hundred years ago Robert Bridges (not yet Poet Laureate) wrote to his younger friend W. B. Yeats, 'I have a new volume of "Collected Works" (a sad sign of age) coming out in October...' Bridges was then a mere 55. To compare small things with great, *Lift Every Heart*, my own first collection of 124 hymn texts, all that I had then written, was published when I was 57. This was followed, roughly at four-year intervals, by three small supplementary collections. There then began to arise in my mind the need for a new 'collected edition', which would contain more than twice the number of texts of *Lift Every Heart*—and this is where Tolstoy comes in.

When contemplating a definitive collected edition, and at the same time still writing a few texts a year, the problem is to know just when to collect. It would be easier if one planned at that point to stop writing, but I hoped to continue for a little. Robert Bridges may have thought it 'a sad sign of age' to be working on such an edition at 55; I was by this time well into my seventies—and Tolstoy's tale was much in my mind.

It seems likely that the heart of Pahóm's story, 'How much land does a man need?', stems from an old folk-legend common to many rural peoples, which Tolstoy took and embellished. In his tale, Pahóm is in search of more land. His travels take him to a nomadic community: 'the people lived on the steppes, by a river, in felt-covered tents.' Here he is told he cannot simply buy land by the acre or *desyatína*, but he can claim for himself as much land as he can walk round between sunrise and sunset. The land is sold by the day, one thousand roubles a day. If he fails to close the boundary by sunset, the price is forfeit.

One can guess the rest. Pahóm strides out, and all morning is delighted at how much land he is encircling. The afternoon wears on, finding him by now tired, still far from where he began, and sun beginning to decline. The last mile or so he has to run faster and faster, some of it uphill. He gains his land and dies in the attempt. How much land did he need then? 'Six feet from his head to his heels'.

I did not want to be like Pahóm, always wanting to add a few more texts before closing the list in a collected edition, to find that I had left it too late and could not see it through the press. So I chose instead to reckon that if I went on writing, I might do as I did with *Lift Every Heart*, and add a future supplement. It was less tidy—but with Pahóm in mind, more sure. So *A House of Praise*, with 285 texts, closed for press at the end of 2001 and was published in 2003; which means that the texts in this present collection were written in the four years 2002–2005. It shares its format with the earlier supplements to *Lift Every Heart*: *Songs of Deliverance*, 1988; *A Voice of Singing*, 1993; and *Great is the Glory*, 1997; because it stands in just the same relationship to *A House of Praise* as they do to *Lift Every Heart*. That book, with its three supplements, went out of print when the hymn texts were subsumed in *A House of Praise*; though *Lift Every Heart* contains some early verse and a couple of introductory essays which have not been reprinted in later books.

As with all my earlier collections, this one includes a few seasonal texts. Christmas has the most because I write some verses each year for our family Christmas card; but there are new texts for Passiontide and Easter, and a number which might prove suitable for Ascensiontide or Trinity Sunday. A new title for me is 'The Meeting' (of Simeon and Anna with the new-born Christ), celebrated in the Church of England as 'The Presentation of Christ in the Temple' forty days after Christmas; there is also a new text based on the Lord's Prayer, and a couple derived from the opening Exhortations at Morning and Evening Prayer.

The publications of the Hymn Society in the United States and Canada sometimes include information about 'hymn searches', often by a local church looking for a new hymn for a special occasion or anniversary. Some few of the texts that follow owe their inspiration to such requests which are often useful as a spur to creativity, whether or not the result proves to be what the church in question is seeking. Along with these go particular commissions, such as 'Our Father God who gave us birth' (wanted for a funeral, hopefully still long in the future); or 'Christ pours his grace upon his own', at the request of a composer. There are two hymns on their patronal saints for churches nearer home, St

Andrew and St Mary Magdalene; and a commission by a City Livery Company for its tercentenary in 2009. 'To Joseph of Nazareth' was not a commission but his day is observed in the Church of England during March, and few hymns are available to choose from. Besides these, a glance will show that I am still on occasion seeking to base new hymns on specific books or passages of the Bible. Psalms are an obvious case in point (this book brings my total to over fifty such texts); and following the examples of Watts and Wesley and many others I offer here two texts from the same short psalm in different metres. As the Notes explain, I wrote three, but two seem enough to publish here. The third can be found, with new tunes by Maurice Bevan to all three, in his *Eight Hymns, set 2* (Cathedral Music, King Charles Cottage, Racton, Chichester, England, PO18 9DT, 2004).

The major prophets have always been an inspiration to hymn writers; for example 'O for a heart to praise my God' by Charles Wesley on Ezekiel 36.26, or 'Bright the vision' by Richard Mant on Isaiah 6. Two texts in this collection spring from those sources: 'O Spirit of the Sovereign Lord' from Isaiah and 'Through stormy cloud and darkness deep' from Ezekiel. Back in the late autumn of 2000 I tried my hand at a cycle of four texts celebrating the writers of the Gospels, Matthew, Mark, Luke and John. I am now in process of doing something of the same for what are known, slightly disparagingly perhaps, as 'the minor prophets', who wrote between them the last twelve books of the Old Testament. The treatment varies, of course, from taking a single verse as a starting point to making the thrust of the whole short book the theme of a hymn. One such was already in print, since in 1984 I wrote 'Behold a broken world, we pray' (one of my very few texts translated into Japanese) to include Micah's famous vision of swords to ploughshares, spears to pruning hooks, 'neither shall they learn war any more'. In this present collection, working backwards from Malachi, I have now reached Micah. Jonah, Obadiah, Amos, Joel and Hosea must await a further book—supposing that, with Pahóm in mind, I am able to complete what I have begun.

Exactly a century ago George Adam Smith was about to publish his celebrated *The Book of the Twelve Prophets,* explaining that they share a common title and unity in the Hebrew Bible as 'The Book of the Twelve' (no mention of 'minor' here!). He describes how these twelve authors

> bring forth and speed on their way not a few of the streams
> of living water which have nourished later ages, and are
> flowing today. Impetuous cataracts of righteousness—*let it*

roll on like water, and justice as an everlasting stream; the irre-pressible love of God to sinful men; the perseverance and pursuits of His grace; His mercies that follow the exile and the outcast; His truth that goes forth richly upon the heathen; the hope of the Saviour of mankind; the outpouring of the Spirit; counsels of patience; impulses of tenderness and of healing; melodies innumerable,—all sprang from these lower hills of prophecy, and sprang so strongly that the world hears and feels them still.

I hope that perhaps some reader of these words, or of the texts that follow, may want to turn again to that portion of their Bible. As with the lady who enjoyed *Hamlet* 'because it was full of quotations', these books provide a rich vein of familiar and often precious verses, even if memory does not always identify the exact writer—and of course I have been able in my texts to allude to or echo only a few of them. Memorably, it was to Habakkuk that John Newton turned on the death of his dear wife Polly in 1790; they had been together for nearly forty years. Newton wrote in his journal: 'On 15th December the Lord released her from all her sorrows. I was watching over her with a can-dle in my hand and saw her draw her last breath.' John Pollock (*Amazing Grace*, London, 1981) continues the story:

He insisted on preaching the next Sunday, saying 'Dr. Pulpit is my best physician.' And he preached at her funeral, from a text, Habakkuk 3:17, 18, which he had reserved, unused, for the day of his greatest affliction, should he outlive her: 'Although the fig tree shall not blossom, neither shall fruit be in the vines; the labour of the olive shall fail, and the fields shall yield no meat; the flock shall be cut off from the fold, and there shall be no herd in the stalls: yet I will rejoice in the Lord, I will joy in the God of my salvation.'

The same verses, as John Pollock points out, were used by Newton's friend William Cowper to conclude No. XLVIII of book 3 of his Olney hymns, under the title *Joy and Peace in Believing:*

The vine, nor fig-tree neither,
    Their wonted fruit should bear,
Though all the fields should wither,
    Nor flocks, nor herds, be there:
Yet God the same abiding,
    His praise shall tune my voice;
For while in him confiding,
    I cannot but rejoice.

Such a familiar example is two-edged for the contemporary hymn writer. It shows what treasures lie in these often neglected short books; but is at the same time daunting in its felicity.

Philip Larkin wrote in one of his reviews (*Philip Larkin: Further Requirements*, ed. Anthony Thwaite, London, 2001) of 'the old gentleman who deleted from his prayer book all expressions praising God, in the belief that they would be distasteful to that well-bred Person'. And if from the incomparable *Book of Common Prayer*, how much more from the greater part of all our hymn books? How dare we, I sometimes ask myself, and with what presumption do we, offer what flows from such pens as ours to be the vehicle for the praise of God? Some of what is sung in worship is unattractive to me: how much more might all that we have to offer be, in Larkin's words, 'distasteful' to Almighty God?

Thoughts such as these might silence human hymnody for ever, were it not for two considerations. The first I owe (as so much else) to Derek Kidner. Writing of high praise offered to God, as we find it in Psalm 48, he says: 'His *praise* is both the renown he deserves, and the response it awakes.' At its best, our praise is almost involuntary, an inescapable response to those glimpses of faith that make up, for most of us, our vision of God. Praise is a necessity for us. It is in the nature of fallen humanity that the attempt falls immeasurably short of its true object; but we can only offer the very best that is in us. Even so, this places a heavy responsibility on those who write for public worship.

The second consideration rests on one of the most remarkable statements of the Gospels. In his conversation with the woman of Samaria at Jacob's Well, Jesus answered the woman's question as to whether worship should be offered 'on this mountain' or in Jerusalem with the words (my italics): 'The hour is coming, and now is, when the true worshippers will worship the Father in spirit and in truth, *for such the Father seeks to worship him.*' If indeed the Father *seeks* our worship (and, on the authority of the Lord Jesus Christ, there is no room for doubt) then, however inadequately, we must respond. In other aspects of my Christian ministry I have often taken comfort from Article XXVI of the Thirty-nine Articles of the Church of England:

> *Of the Unworthiness of the Ministers, which hinders not the effect of the Sacrament.* Although in the visible Church the evil be ever mingled with the good, and sometimes the evil have chief authority in the Ministration of the Word and Sacraments, yet forasmuch as they do not the same in their own name, but in Christ's, and do minister by his commis-

sion and authority, we may use their Ministry, both in hearing the Word of God, and in the receiving of the Sacraments
...which be effectual, because of Christ's institution and
promise, although they be ministered by evil men.

In something of the same way, I like to feel that the unworthiness of the
vehicle through which a congregation sing their praise 'hinders not the
effect' in the sight of God. Two consequences seem to follow. First, that
the 'vehicle' should not presume on this gracious provision, but should
be the very best that we can offer. Not all our hymn texts will be, or even
should be Rolls Royces; but they should all be decently roadworthy, and
as true to Scripture, as free from blemish, as carefully constructed, as
appealing to imagination, heart and will, and as user-friendly as we can
make them. The fact that God deigns to accept our human efforts, and
to bring good even out of their deficiencies, is no mandate for a casual
approach to our work. Theresa Whistler, writing of Walter de la Mare
(*The Imagination of the Heart,* London, 1993), quotes his letter to a corre-
spondent: 'I don't believe *you* really know what downright *gruelling* at a
poem means.' The word implies what is exhausting, even punishing. If
such a draftsman as de la Mare looked for that in the writing of poetry,
how much more in liturgy and hymns? Of course, after all our efforts,
our work will be unworthy. Yet, as with Article XXVI above, God will
bring strength out of weakness. And Bernard Lord Manning offered in
his *The Hymns of Wesley and Watts* (London, 1942) a salutary reminder
that good taste and literary merit are not everything:

> Reverence is due to hymns as to any sacred object. The hymn
> that revolts me, if it has been a means of grace to Christian
> men, I must respect as I should respect a communion cup,
> however scratched its surface, however vulgar its decoration.

* * * * *

As with my earlier collections, the Index of Biblical References on page
67 contains only those verses or passages which form the theme of a
hymn, or of a distinct portion of one; and does not set out to be a com-
prehensive list of Biblical allusions or quotations. Sharp-eyed readers
may note that there is no Cumulative Index of Subjects or of First Lines,
since both these appeared in full in *A House of Praise;* the Indexes there,
taken together with those at the end of this book, form a complete
record of all my texts to date. There is also no need of an Index of
Hymnals, since only one of these hymns has found a place in a published hymnal to date, and this was thanks to remarkably speedy work
by the hymnal's editors: see the Note on 'The final triumph won'.

With much thankfulness I record my debt to Jane Emden, who transferred my manuscript to a word-processor; and to the two physicians, Dr. Peter Tucker and Dr. Jonathan West, now retired from practice, who have given me unstinted counsel and suggestions for suitable tunes, though the responsibility for the choices shown rests with me. As readers of *A House of Praise* may remember from the Preface, it has long been agreed that Oxford University Press will become the administrators of my hymn copyrights, in territories not served by the Hope Publishing Company, at some future date; and this has now been fixed as 1 January 2007. In the meantime I offer renewed thanks to these publishers and to all whose help has made possible both *A House of Praise* and this new supplement to it.

T.D.S.

Ford, 2005

THE HYMNS

The hymn texts are not numbered, but are listed in alphabetical order both here and in the notes (pages 39–63). An Index of First Lines is included for easy reference at the back of the book (page 76).

A RIGHTEOUS GOD IN HEAVEN REIGNS

based on Nahum 1

A righteous God in heaven reigns,
against his foes his arm is strong:
his throne the rule of right maintains,
his justice will avenge the wrong.

He rides the whirlwind, storm and gale,
about his feet the lightnings play;
the seas are dry, the rivers fail,
the mountains melt like wax away.

His righteous indignations burn;
as fire and flame his wrath is poured:
in judgment swift the guilty learn
the day of vengeance of the Lord.

*

Our God is good! His mercy stands:
unwearied love is still the same.
We rest in his eternal hands
with all who trust his holy Name.

Behold, upon the mountain height
the herald's cry awakes the morn!
The darkness flees before the light,
and our redemption's day is born.

ALMIGHTY FATHER, GOD OF GRACE

Almighty Father, God of grace,
    to whom in love your children pray,
we worship here before your face
    and give you thanks for yesterday;
for all who shared our hopes and fears,
    who tread with joy that farther shore:
we pause amid the passing years
    to honour those now gone before.

Their love of justice guide our ways,
    the fires of freedom in us burn;
may we, with them, our Maker praise,
    and share his gospel in our turn.
O Spirit, shine upon the word,
    your gifts of life and truth impart:
the call of God again be heard
    and courage rise in every heart.

Let love and peace unite our powers
    in joyful songs with one accord;
a covenant of grace is ours,
    to walk as one before the Lord:
and, one in Christ, together find
    in him the Truth that makes us free,
one family in heart and mind
    for all the years that are to be.

ANGELIC HOSTS ABOVE

based on Psalm 89.5–18

Angelic hosts above
   the Lord of glory praise,
his faithfulness and love
   from everlasting days.
      His Name declare
         in earth and sky!
      With God Most High
         who can compare?

How awesome his decrees,
   his mighty hand displayed!
He calms the raging seas
   and rules the worlds he made.
      From nature's night
         he brought to birth
      the founded earth,
         the starry height.

Before his judgment seat,
   where justice rules alone,
his truth and mercy meet,
   the pillars of his throne.
      Supreme he reigns,
         who by his power
      from hour to hour
         the world sustains.

Secure beneath his care
   rejoice to walk his way,
and in his presence share
   the light of heaven's day.
      His Name adored,
         to faith revealed,
      is King and Shield
         and glorious Lord!

For Europe and Africa: © Timothy Dudley-Smith
For the rest of the world including the USA and Canada: © 2006 Hope Publishing Company

AS JESUS TAUGHT US, FIRST WE PRAY

based on the Lord's Prayer,
Matthew 6.5–13

As Jesus taught us, first we pray
your Name be hallowed day by day,
   Father in heaven.

Then, for our world of sin and pain,
hasten the hour when Christ shall reign:
   your kingdom come.

Move in our hearts that wars may cease:
Author of justice, truth and peace,
   your will be done.

Lord of the fruitful earth you made,
give to us all, who seek your aid,
   our daily bread.

Grant us in Christ the hope of heaven;
and, as we seek to be forgiven,
   help us forgive.

From the assaults of evil's power,
and in the soul's unguarded hour,
   save us, good Lord.

Yours is the kingdom, power and praise,
glory be yours from endless days,
   for evermore!

AT THE THRONE OF GRACE

before worship

At the throne of grace
let us seek God's face,
all our sins and griefs confessing,
longing only for his blessing,
    as in holy fear
    we in faith draw near.

Let us hear his voice
and in hope rejoice:
word of promise now believing,
word of pardon here receiving,
    word of love unpriced
    from the lips of Christ.

May our hearts be stirred
and our prayers be heard:
may our worship and thanksgiving
lead us on to holy living,
    as we seek God's face
    at his throne of grace.

For Europe and Africa: © Timothy Dudley-Smith
For the rest of the world including the USA and Canada: © 2006 Hope Publishing Company

BEYOND WHAT MIND CAN MEASURE

Beyond what mind can measure
    or human heart disclose,
in Christ there lies the treasure
    that only wisdom knows.
His word of life discerning,
    we stand on holy ground;
where, written for our learning,
    eternal truth is found.

A world of warring nations
    denies what God has willed:
for Christless generations
    their dreams are unfulfilled.
In learning, Lord, and teaching,
    may we our powers assign
to meet the minds outreaching
    in quest of life divine.

To hearts whose hope is sinking,
    to spirits bleak and bare,
to thought itself, where thinking
    is meaningless despair,
reveal again your glory,
    O God of grace and power,
and help us tell your story
    in ways to match the hour.

May he who died to save us
    renew the love we claim,
to spend the gifts he gave us
    in service of his Name;
till truth at last prevailing,
    in Christ the nations find
the Light and Life unfailing
    of every heart and mind.

BREAK INTO GLAD EXULTANT SONG

based on Zephaniah 3.12–20

Break into glad exultant song,
    forgiven, loved, and blessed;
released from old familiar wrong,
    in God rejoice and rest.

Let fears and foes alike depart
    before his state and throne;
his peace possess the anxious heart
    where Christ is loved and known.

The Lord exults in those who trust,
    he heals our sin and shame;
he lifts our spirits from the dust
    to glory in his Name.

He gathers in his wayward flock,
    to life and joy restored;
he sets our feet upon the rock,
    the ransomed of the Lord.

In God is all his people's praise,
    his Name their high renown,
himself their home to endless days,
    our glory and our crown.

CHRIST POURS HIS GRACE UPON HIS OWN

C hrist pours his grace upon his own,
and where the word of life is sown
there shall the fruits of grace be grown:
to him be glory, whose cross and passion
have bought and saved us; to him be glory.

God's changeless love shall never fail.
Though powers of sin and death assail,
his purpose stands and shall prevail:
to him be glory, our great Creator,
eternal Father, to him be glory.

Come, Spirit, then and make us one.
Fulfil your work of grace begun:
and now as Father, Spirit, Son,
to God be glory from us his children,
throughout all ages, to God be glory.

GIVE THANKS TO GOD ABOVE

based on Psalm 107

Give thanks to God above
  and make his glories known,
the Father whose redeeming love
  still gathers in his own.

In deserts of despair,
  when faint and far astray,
the Lord himself will meet us there
  and be himself the Way.

In darkness and distress,
  and rebels though we be,
he hears us in our helplessness
  and sets the prisoner free.

In weight of sin laid low,
  by sickness sore oppressed,
the weary still his welcome know,
  and taste his promised rest.

In storm, and tempest-tossed,
  when waves as mountains come,
he stills the seas and leads the lost
  to haven and to home.

All things are in his hand:
  rejoice in him who reigns!
For evermore his mercies stand,
  his steadfast love remains.

GLORY TO GOD, AND PRAISE

Glory to God, and praise:
    exalt his holy Name!
the Ancient of eternal Days
    from age to age the same.
The whole created earth
    proclaims his sovereign power,
whose love has brought us from our birth
    to serve this present hour.

Glory to God the Son,
    who laid aside his crown:
by wood and nails his work was done
    who came in mercy down.
The hands that made the hills
    took chisel, saw and plane,
and hallowed all our human skills
    of heart and hand and brain.

Glory to God on high
    whose Spirit gives us breath.
Our life in him shall never die,
    his love has conquered death.
May we his presence know:
    descend in power, we pray!
O Wind of God, from heaven blow
    about our world today.

Glory to God, who reigns
    all thrones and powers above,
whose arm the sum of things sustains
    in righteousness and love.
When earthly days are done
    and shadows fade and flee,
then still to Father, Spirit, Son,
    our endless praise shall be!

'GLORY TO THE GOD OF HEAVEN'

'Glory to the God of heaven,
peace on earth to mortals given':
    hear again the angel's voice!
Promised hope of every nation,
Christ has come for our salvation,
    let the waiting world rejoice!

Word of God beyond our telling,
Son of God with sinners dwelling,
    God appears in human frame:
flesh and blood their Maker borrows,
born to bear our griefs and sorrows,
    who as Love incarnate came.

Love enshrined in infant tender,
blazoned forth in heaven's splendour,
    King of love to earth come down:
God in Christ among us living,
tasting death for our forgiving,
    bowed beneath a thorny crown.

To this child of our salvation
join the songs of adoration,
    hear again the angels' cry!
Christ is risen, Christ ascended,
all our sins and sorrows ended:
    Glory be to God Most High!

HALLOW THE FATHER'S NAME

Hallow the Father's Name!
Through all our hopes and fears
his heart of love is still the same
    amid the changing years:
who formed us in his grace
    and keeps us by his power,
who calls his church to seek his face
    and serve this present hour.

Glory to Christ the Son,
    the Prince of life who died,
the Servant who salvation won,
    the Saviour glorified!
Teach us to hear his call
    and tell his truth abroad,
who gave himself to save us all
    and reigns our risen Lord.

Welcome the Spirit blest,
    whose fruitful gifts increase
the grace of God made manifest
    in love and joy and peace!
A new resolve impart
    to serve our neighbours' need,
intent to bind the broken heart
    and see the captive freed.

Honour and power and might,
    dominion, love and praise,
be unto him who reigns in light
    through everlasting days:
from earth to realms above,
    from sea to starlit sky,
exalt one Trinity of love
    in majesty on high!

HOW DARK THE NIGHT OF CLOUD AND CARES

based on Psalm 3

How dark the night of cloud and cares,
a sky without a star,
when doubts arise to mock my prayers,
and God seems far.

Come, then, and make your presence known
in joy and faith restored.
My hope is set on God alone:
be near me, Lord.

The Lord is my encircling shield,
a glory round me shed;
in love and power alike revealed,
he lifts my head.

He hears me from his throne on high,
beneath his hand I sleep;
and he who answers every cry
his watch will keep.

The Lord will take his people's part!
In him, beloved and blest,
the peace of God possess my heart:
in him I rest.

For Europe and Africa: © Timothy Dudley-Smith
For the rest of the world including the USA and Canada: © 2006 Hope Publishing Company

HOW HAPPY THOSE INDEED

based on Psalm 1

How happy those indeed
who turn from evil's way,
resolved to give no heed
   to what the world may say:
     who do not walk
      where sin is near
      nor meet to hear
     the scorners' talk.

In God is their delight,
   for them his voice is heard;
they ponder day and night
   on his unchanging word.
     What gift unpriced
      his law imparts
      to lead their hearts
     to follow Christ!

The righteous are as trees
   where living waters flow:
how fair and fruitful these,
   who prosper as they grow!
     So strong they stand,
      for evil fails
      and right prevails
     beneath God's hand!

HOW HAPPY THOSE WHO WALK IN TRUTH

based on Psalm 1

How happy those who walk in truth,
nor make the wrong their choice,
nor take the path that sinners tread,
nor sit where scornful words are said,
but in the law of God are led
    to wonder and rejoice.

The meditations of their heart
    by day and night incline
to ponder God's eternal word
and find, with soul and conscience stirred,
the very voice of God is heard,
    a law of life divine.

As trees beside the water stand
    in summer's splendour seen,
and nourished by the streams that flow
their ripened fruits in season show,
so shall the godly thrive and grow,
    whose leaves are always green.

The wicked fly like scattered chaff
    upon the wind away:
the Lord shall drive them forth as dust,
but those who in his mercy trust
await the mansions of the just
    in everlasting day.

IN THE STILLNESS, HARK!

In the stillness, hark!
Through the silent dark
comes a sound of angels singing,
comes a voice from heaven bringing
news of peace on earth
through a Saviour's birth.

Here by faith behold
Jesus, long foretold.
In this infant here reclining,
by whose light the stars are shining,
we have seen and heard
God's incarnate Word.

Not with kingly crown
does our God come down:
but our human flesh he borrows,
Friend of sinners, Man of sorrows,
for our life to die,
in our grave to lie.

From that grave again
he arose to reign!
He who lay, by Mary tended,
is the Prince of life ascended,
honoured, loved, adored,
he is Christ the Lord!

For Europe and Africa: © Timothy Dudley-Smith
For the rest of the world including the USA and Canada: © 2006 Hope Publishing Company

JESUS CHRIST IS BORN TODAY

Jesus Christ is born today,
 Every heart its homage pay!
Sovereign Prince of David's line,
Universal King divine!
Songs of glory greet the morn,
 Alleluia, Christ is born!

Christ the Lamb of God behold:
He of whom the prophets told,
Royal babe of humble birth,
Infant Judge of all the earth!
Sing of that momentous morn,
Thanking God that Christ is born.

In the manger there you lie,
Son of Mary, born to die,
Born for us, to seek and save,
Only Lord of death and grave;
Raised to life on Easter morn:
Night is over! Christ is born!

Through your cross are sins forgiven,
Open stands the gate of heaven!
Down the years to you we bring
All our praise, ascended King!
Yours the songs of Christmas morn:
 Alleluia, Christ is born!

LIGHT OF THE WORLD, TRUE LIGHT DIVINE

Light of the world,
      true light divine,
in glory break
      and splendour shine
            upon our nature's night!
The darkness dies
      before the morn
and God himself
      a child is born,
            the long-awaited Light.

Life of the world,
      a life laid down,
who chose the cross
      before the crown
            and opened heaven's door:
he broke the chains
      of death and hell,
our Saviour Christ,
      Emmanuel,
            who lives for evermore.

Lord of all worlds,
      a manger bed
was room enough
      to lay your head
            when, from your throne above,
you came to set
      a lost world right,
immortal Life,
      unfading Light,
            and all-prevailing Love.

NOT OURS TO KNOW THE REASONS

based on the Book of Haggai

Not ours to know the reasons
for all that God has planned,
the days and times and seasons
secure within his hand.
From days of drought unbroken,
of harvests unfulfilled,
the Lord himself has spoken:
there comes a time to build.

From sins that yet enslave us,
from love grown faint and cold,
be swift, O Lord, to save us,
draw near us as of old.
In mercy, peace and blessing
your love be shed abroad,
our hearts of hearts possessing,
the temple of the Lord.

What tongue can tell the story,
or sing Messiah's worth,
the Christ who comes in glory
to shake the powers of earth?
Exalt him, all creation,
the Lamb for sinners slain,
desire of every nation
in God's eternal reign!

O GOD, FROM AGE TO AGE THE SAME

based on the prayer of Habakkuk, chapter 3

O God, from age to age the same,
   while nations rise and pass away,
enthroned beyond renown or fame,
   look down in pity as we pray,
and for the greatness of your Name
   revive your work in this our day.

Your splendour shines in earth and sky,
   there flashes lightning from your hand,
the mountains shake, the floods are high,
   before your presence who can stand?
In God we trust: O hear our cry,
   and stoop to save our broken land.

Though every tree be bare of leaf
   and blossoms fall to frost and hail,
though corn lie blackened in the sheaf
   and flocks decline and harvests fail,
yet hope shall triumph over grief
   and death itself shall not prevail.

In God rejoice, our strength and stay,
   our Saviour, Judge, and faithful friend;
exult in him from day to day
   whatever change and chance may send.
His love will still direct our way
   and bring us safe to journey's end.

O GOD OF PEACE, WHO GAVE US BREATH AND BIRTH

for the peace of the world

O God of peace, who gave us breath and birth,
　　our life, our powers, and all good gifts beside,
look down in mercy on this troubled earth
　　where want and war and hatred still divide.
　　　　So move our hearts, O Lord, to work and pray
　　　　that peace may yet prevail in this our day.

O Saviour Christ, as Prince of peace you came,
　　draw near in power to those who hear your call,
who, making peace, bring honour to your Name,
　　and on their labours let your blessing fall.
　　　　As to your friends you chose your peace to leave,
　　　　so may our world your life and peace receive.

O Spirit blest, the gift of God above,
　　your holy influence on our hearts increase;
bring forth in us your fruit of joy and love,
　　unite your people in the bond of peace.
　　　　Give strength to build afresh, to right the wrongs,
　　　　and seek that peace for which creation longs.

God grant us wisdom, peaceable and pure,
　　lift up on us your countenance, O Lord;
so may the strong be just, the weak secure,
　　and nations learn at last to sheathe the sword.
　　　　Bestow through Christ the peace of sins forgiven,
　　　　that all the earth may be at peace with heaven.

O GOD THE JUST, ENTHRONED ON HIGH

based on Malachi 3 & 4

O God the Just, enthroned on high,
　　whose balance weighs our right and wrong,
before your judgment seat we cry,
　　how long, O Lord, how long?

Shall villainy and vice prevail,
　　corruption lead the weak astray?
How long till powers of darkness fail,
　　how long, O Lord, till day?

The Lord will come! Through timeless years
　　his covenant is still the same:
but who can stand when he appears,
　　for holy is his Name?

His mercy bids the lost return
　　and, freed from all their former ways,
with hearts renewed begin to learn
　　their sacrifice of praise.

Our lives we bring to serve the Lord,
　　our minds be set on things above;
and ours, from heaven's windows poured,
　　the blessings of his love.

Until at last, with wondering eyes,
　　we see, what all creation sings,
the Sun of Righteousness arise
　　with healing in his wings.

O GOD, WHOSE THRONE ETERNAL STANDS

O God, whose throne eternal stands,
    we lift our hearts in praise;
the passing years are in your hands,
    the measure of our days.
We come with songs before your face,
    your mercies here confess,
recount your acts of saving grace,
    declare your faithfulness.

Created from the dust of earth
    and by the Spirit's breath,
your love was ours before our birth,
    your life shall conquer death.
We praise with all who in your sight
    have passed this way before,
and now rejoice in greater light
    upon a farther shore.

We tread today the path they trod,
    their covenant we claim;
we join with them in praise of God
    unchangeably the same.
More constant than the stars above
    there stands the gift unpriced,
the pledge of never-failing love,
    your Son, our Saviour Christ.

Let joy be ours, who journey still
    to futures yet unknown!
We rest within a Father's will,
    where Love is on the throne.
To God and to the Threefold Name
    all praise and glory be,
our God, unchangeably the same,
    through all eternity!

O SPIRIT OF THE SOVEREIGN LORD

based on Isaiah 61.1–3

O Spirit of the Sovereign Lord,
    descend in power, we pray,
on all who minister your word
    and teach your truth today.

May those whom God has set apart,
    anointed, called and blessed,
announce good news to every heart
    by want or sin oppressed.

Let songs of liberty be sung,
    the lamps of freedom burn;
as wide the prison gates are flung
    forgotten hopes return.

The favour of the Lord proclaim
    in pardon freely given,
for just and righteous is his Name,
    the God of earth and heaven.

May all who mourn, his comfort know;
    their every tear be dried;
as trees of righteousness to grow
    that God be glorified.

O Spirit of the Sovereign Lord,
    descend on us who pray,
renew your church in deed and word
    to serve your world today.

OUR FATHER GOD WHO GAVE US BIRTH

for a funeral

Our Father God who gave us birth
and ordered all our days on earth,
beneath whose hand we live and move,
the ransomed children of his love,
    who gave his Son our griefs to bear,
    be near us now and hear our prayer.

Though shadows fall, our song be praise
for fruitful years and sunlit days;
for surging sea and starry sky
and hearts where love shall never die;
    for life that conquers death and grave,
    where Christ is risen, strong to save.

Beneath his cross our hopes we rest
where death and life alike are blest,
and we who move from dust to dust
in Christ and in his promise trust:
    the Shepherd good, who knows his sheep,
    whose arm has kept them, and will keep.

In Christ shall all our hopes prevail,
no part of all his promise fail;
for he who here our nature shared
has won for us a place prepared,
    to live with him that life to come,
    and find his Father's house our home.

PRINCE OF LIFE AND LORD OF GLORY

Prince of life and Lord of glory,
  to whose Name be love and praise;
Son of God, whose human story
  touches all our earthly days,
    still our guide and teacher be,
    as of old in Galilee.

Crowds who came where Christ was preaching,
  in the hills or by the shore,
wondered at his gracious teaching,
  as no prophet taught before:
    where today your voice is heard
    tune our hearts to hear your word.

Mary's son, on earth revealing
  God himself in word and sign,
toiling, travelling, teaching, healing,
  love incarnate, love divine,
    come as Shepherd of the soul,
    touch our lives and make them whole.

He who came for our befriending,
  selfless Saviour, Son of man,
on the cross at Calvary ending
  all that Bethlehem began,
    Christ, who died to make us free,
    in your love remember me.

Risen Lord in glory seated,
  high-enthroned ascended Son,
sinners ransomed, death defeated,
  all a world's salvation won,
    Prince of life, our lives sustain,
    till with you we rise and reign!

TEACH US YOUR VOICE TO HEAR

based on Mark 12.29–31

Teach us your voice to hear
  and your commands obey;
to serve you, Lord, with godly fear
  and gladly walk your way.

Make love our highest goal:
  this gift of grace impart,
to love the Lord with all our soul
  and mind and strength and heart.

So may our spirits thirst
  to count all neighbours friends,
in loving him who loved us first
  with love that never ends.

THE FINAL TRIUMPH WON

The final triumph won,
   the full atonement made,
salvation's work is done,
     redemption's price is paid:
        the morning breaks, the dark is fled,
        for Christ is risen from the dead!

The tomb in which he lay
    lies empty now and bare;
the stone is rolled away,
     no lifeless form is there:
        the sting is drawn from death and grave,
        for Christ is risen, strong to save!

For us the Saviour died,
    with us he lives again,
to God the Father's side
     exalted now to reign:
        to throne and crown by right restored,
        for Christ is risen, Christ is Lord!

As one with him we rise
    to seek the things above,
in life that never dies,
     in righteousness and love:
        let praise unite our ransomed powers,
        for Christ is risen, Christ is ours!

THE GOD OF WHOM THE PROPHETS TOLD

based on images from the Book of Zechariah

The God of whom the prophets told,
  when truth in signs and visions came,
we now in Christ by faith behold
  and hear his word and know his Name.

That Name the ransomed glorify,
  by God redeemed, a burning brand,
the apple of our Maker's eye,
  the jewels shining in his hand.

No longer shepherdless we roam,
  the flock for whom the Saviour died,
the Lord shall make with us his home
  and be our light at eventide.

His grace alone our confidence,
  his Spirit's power about our ways,
a wall of fire our sure defence,
  his covenant our song of praise.

Rejoice! for Christ shall come again,
  with peace and righteousness restored:
from sea to sea our King shall reign,
  and all be holy to the Lord.

THE PROMISED LIGHT OF ALL THE EARTH

based on Luke 2.22–38
The Presentation of Christ in the Temple

The promised Light of all the earth
    is sprung from David's line,
and in his long-awaited birth
    salvation's glories shine.

We share by faith the gift of grace
    to favoured Simeon given,
who saw his Saviour's infant face
    and blessed the God of heaven.

We know, what he foresaw in part,
    the coming cross and grave,
a sword to pierce through Mary's heart,
    a life laid down to save.

So we with Anna stand and bless
    and lift our hearts above,
to tell in praise and thankfulness
    of God's redeeming love.

O Lord our God, we here present
    our sacrifice of praise,
and offer up the life you lent,
    the service of our days.

Be ours the risen Christ to know
    who to his Temple came,
that meeting him we live and grow
    and glory in his Name.

THOUGH ONE WITH GOD IN FORM DIVINE

based on Philippians 2.6–11

Though one with God in form divine,
by this the love of Christ is shown:
he chose in mercy to resign
his place beside the Father's throne.

He laid his kingly glories down,
in self-surrender stooped to save,
and stripped himself of state and crown
to bear the likeness of a slave.

Intent to do the Father's will,
in human form and flesh he came;
and to the last obedient still
he died in agony and shame.

Till from the dark of death's repose,
the shuttered tomb, the midnight hour,
the Lord of life to glory rose,
exalted by the Father's power.

To him, by God the Father given,
that Name belongs, all names above,
a Name unmatched in earth or heaven
for honour, majesty and love.

His Name let all creation bless,
on bended knees in homage fall;
and to the Father's praise confess
that Jesus Christ is Lord of all!

THROUGH STORMY CLOUD AND DARKNESS DEEP

Through stormy cloud and darkness deep,
   however far afield they roam,
God is the Shepherd of his sheep
   who seeks the lost to bring them home:
      our longing eyes by faith behold
      one flock, one Shepherd and one fold.

To seek and save, to guard and keep,
   his own to nurture and defend,
Christ is the Shepherd of his sheep
   who bears us safe to journey's end:
      our dwelling place, through endless days,
      in God's eternal house of praise.

What though the path be long and steep,
   and some are faint, or far astray?
Christ gives new shepherds to his sheep
   to tend the flock of God today:
      his word to teach, his church to build,
      and see his purposes fulfilled.

Those loving purposes remain,
   more constant than the stars above:
beyond our earthbound sin and pain
   he leads the children of his love
      with joy to stand before his throne,
      and know as we are loved and known.

TO GOD BE GLORY, LOVE AND PRAISE

Mary Magdalene

To God be glory, love and praise,
for all his saints of other days
    who built this house of prayer;
who sought within its walls a home
where all alike may freely come,
    and find a welcome there.

For troubled hearts it tells of peace,
to those in bondage brings release,
    like Mary Magdalene;
who found in Christ a friend indeed,
and at his word was healed and freed
    from all the powers of sin.

So may our hearts, like Mary's, burn
to love and serve him in return,
    and in his love abide;
content to reckon all things loss
and watch with her at Jesus' cross
    where Love was crucified.

Her joy be ours, as from the grave
she met the one who died to save
    triumphantly restored;
we hear with her the Saviour's voice
and in his endless life rejoice,
    our risen, reigning Lord!

TO GOD MOST HIGH BE GIVEN

before worship

To God Most High be given
　　the sacrifice of praise,
the songs of earth and heaven,
　　the service of our days.
Our secret sins confessing
　　in penitence and shame,
we find a Father's blessing
　　through our Redeemer's Name.

With open hearts, believing,
　　with mind and conscience stirred,
the truth of God receiving,
　　we hear his holy word.
For neighbour, church and nation,
　　a world of human need,
in common supplication
　　we join to intercede.

May God the Spirit guide us,
　　his presence here be known;
our Saviour stand beside us
　　to make our prayers his own.
With thankfulness unmeasured
　　his mercies we recall,
by Love beloved and treasured
　　who loved and made us all.

TO JOSEPH OF NAZARETH GOD GAVE INTEGRITY

To Joseph of Nazareth God gave integrity,
David's descendant of Abraham's line;
for Mary and Jesus a husband and guardian,
chosen to cherish a Saviour divine.

When Joseph of Nazareth worked for his family,
earning their living by things that he made,
he fostered in Jesus the skills of his craftsmanship,
teaching our Maker a carpenter's trade.

Be Joseph of Nazareth honoured in memory,
patiently working till Jesus had grown;
through years of obscurity hidden in Galilee,
loving as father a son not his own.

For Joseph of Nazareth, shaper of destiny,
nurturing Jesus from earliest days,
to God who is Father and Saviour and Strengthener,
thanks be for Joseph, and honour and praise!

For Europe and Africa: © Timothy Dudley-Smith
For the rest of the world including the USA and Canada: © 2006 Hope Publishing Company

WHAT SENSE OF NEED LED ANDREW ON

St Andrew

What sense of need led Andrew on,
  what longings, none but he could say,
to be baptized and follow John
    in search of life and truth and way.
When John announced the one foretold
    that long-awaited word sufficed:
'Behold the Lamb of God, behold!'
    and Andrew turned to follow Christ.

In Christ he found the truth he sought,
    a way to walk, a life restored,
a faith to share, as first he brought
    his brother Peter to the Lord.
They left their nets by Galilee
    to be of Jesus' twelve a part,
and sail for him a vaster sea
    as fishers of the human heart.

They fed the flock, as once were fed
    the crowds who sat at Jesus' feet,
who watched him take the fish and bread
    and give the hungry food to eat.
Today we honour Andrew still,
    who made the cause of Christ his own,
and seek his calling to fulfil
    who lived to make his Master known.

NOTES ON THE HYMNS

In these Notes the following abbreviations are used for versions of the Bible:

AV *Authorized Version,* 1611, also known as the *King James Version*
RV *Revised Version,* 1881–5
RSV *Revised Standard Version,* 1946–52
JBP *J. B. Phillips,* 1958
JB *Jerusalem Bible,* 1958
NEB *New English Bible,* 1970
NIV *New International Version,* 1979
REB *Revised English Bible,* 1989
NRSV *New Revised Standard Version,* 1990

Knox refers to the translation by Ronald A. Knox, 1946–9

Gelineau refers to the translation arranged for singing to the psalmody of Joseph Gelineau, 1963

Note also:
ASB *Alternative Service Book, 1980*
BCP *Book of Common Prayer,* 1662

A RIGHTEOUS GOD IN HEAVEN REIGNS   88 88 (LM) *or*
                                                88 888 (LM extended)

Based on	Nahum 1
Theme	God the Father; judgment; Advent
Written	at Ford, November 2004
Suggested tune	GONFALON ROYAL by Percy Buck
	NIAGARA by Robert Jackson
	ST DROSTANE by J. B. Dykes
	TORQUAY by William Youens
	WINCHESTER NEW adapted by Henry Havergal

In 1984 I wrote a hymn drawing on some well-known verses from the book of Micah, one of the twelve 'minor prophets' of the Old Testament. It appears as No. 272 in *A House of Praise*, 'Behold a broken world, we pray'. Some time later, as the Foreword explains, I thought that I would try to see whether there was not a new hymn to be written from some part of each of these prophecies, and the present text comes from a reading of the book of Nahum. The book has only three chapters, almost entirely concerned with the sack of Nineveh, which was to fall in 612 BC. In his vision Nahum speaks with 'the voice of an outraged conscience'; but hymnody differs from prophecy. I have tried therefore to be true to the thrust of the book, and its vision of a righteous (and offended) God, while offering a hymn suitable for Christian worship. The occasions when it would be the right choice of hymn are probably few; though it could well mark the traditional solemnity of Advent, to set alongside the note of joyful expectation. Perhaps, too, we shall live to see the return of days when public worship includes formal national (if not international) penitence for our behaviour towards God, towards each other, and towards God's created order.

The asterisk is intended to indicate a change of mood as between the two 'days' which conclude verses 3 and 5. Sung by a choir, or following a congregational practice, it could well be marked by some bars of music unaccompanied, to give time for reflection before the singing starts again.

Two further tunes which serve the text well are in the metre LM Extended, and therefore repeat the final line of each verse, a device which helps to emphasize the meaning of the text. TORQUAY (originally CONFIDENCE) dates from the *Primitive Methodist Hymnal Supplement* of 1912 and appears in *Hymns and Psalms* among other collections. BOROUGH LIGHTS by Richard Simpkin can be found in *Praise!*, 2000 to his own words, 'We praise the God in whom we trust'.

ALMIGHTY FATHER, GOD OF GRACE   88 88 D (DLM)

Theme	Anniversary; celebration; mission; unity
Written	at Ford, November 2004
Suggested tune	FIRMAMENT by H. Walford Davies
	LONDON (or ADDISON'S) by John Sheeles

This is a text of celebration, suitable for any milestone, large or small, in the life of a Christian community or church. As a hymn to mark an anniversary, it begins with a glance backwards in respect and gratitude 'for those now gone before'. It moves on, in the second verse, to ask that the worshippers of today may prove worthy of their inheritance of faith; and that God will speak today, as in the past, to call his people to his service in the cause of justice, freedom, and the sharing of the everlasting gospel. And because this is the task of the whole fellowship, the final verse is a prayer for the fruit of the Spirit to be evident in the common life, so that together, as the unknown future is unfolded, the united church may experience the revealed truth and resurrection life of the Lord himself.

In verse 1, the phrase 'that farther shore' as a metaphor for heaven, comes from the crossing of Jordan as an image of death; used memorably by Isaac Watts to conclude his 'There is a land of pure delight'. Much ink has been spilt on the distinction between 'farther' and 'further': I have used 'farther' because distance is implied, but editors are free to change it.

ANGELIC HOSTS ABOVE   6666 4444

Based on	Psalm 89.5–18
Theme	God the Father; praise and worship
Written	at Ford, February 2004
Suggested tune	HAREWOOD by S. S. Wesley

In 1970 when *Psalm Praise* was in preparation I wrote a metrical version of the first 18 verses of this psalm, No. 155 in *A House of Praise*, 'Timeless love! We sing the story'. That was some 35 years ago, years in which it has found its way, usually to Norman Warren's fine tune TIMELESS LOVE, into hymnals not only in the United Kingdom, but in Australia, New Zealand, Hong Kong and the United States.

Reading the psalm one morning, I noticed how self-contained are verses 5–18 from which Derek Kidner (*Psalms 73–150*, London, 1975) expounds the majesty, mastery and moral grandeur of God; and it is this thought which forms the subject of the hymn. The opening line is drawn from the REB translation, 'the assembly of the angels'; while 'earth and sky' looks forward to verse 11 of the psalm, the source also of 'founded'. Shakespeare in *Macbeth* speaks of 'founded as the rock' and it is an image which appealed to Charles Wesley. 'Nature's night' in verse 2 is the primordial darkness of Genesis 1.2; in Wordsworth's phrase, 'breathless Nature's dark abyss'. 'The pillars of his throne' (verse 3) is a direct borrowing from Knox; while 'King and Shield' are the titles the Psalmist uses, in many translations, to conclude this section. 'Glorious Lord' is the phrase chosen by Charles Wesley to conclude his 'A prayer for the Church of England', borrowed, perhaps, from Isaiah 33.21 (AV).

AS JESUS TAUGHT US, FIRST WE PRAY   884

Based on	The Lord's Prayer, Matthew 6.5–13
Theme	Prayer
Written	at Ford, August 2002
Suggested tune	LANTEGLOS by John Dykes Bower

Among my early texts of the 1960s was a metrical paraphrase of the Lord's Prayer, No. 203 in *A House of Praise*, 'Father, who formed the family of man'. This new attempt took its origin from the tune LANTEGLOS which I came across when considering metres to which I had not yet written. The composer was chairman of the board of Hymns Ancient and Modern, and Cyril Taylor in *Hymns for Today Discussed* (Norwich, 1985) confirms that the tune was written to carry Eric Milner-White's text, 'Lord that descendest, Holy Child', No. 398 in *Ancient and Modern New Standard*, a book that subsumes *Hymns for Today:* I have not found the tune in any other collection. Milner-White uses the same refrain at the end of each couplet: but it seemed possible to vary this, and the framework of the Lord's Prayer provides, with a little coaxing, a set of final lines. The hymn seeks to follow the traditional wording, though with no specific reference to 'trespasses', and avoids the choice between 'temptation' and 'time of trial'. 'Hallowed' (which I see as a technical term rather than an archaic one) remains in all the versions of the Prayer to be found in *Common Worship*, 2000 and its counterparts from many other English-speaking churches.

'Author' in verse 3 looks more, perhaps, to the *Book of Common Prayer* ('...Author of peace and lover of concord...') than to the AV (where the word is used of the Lord Jesus Christ, Hebrews 12.2) but the sense seems to me secure. 'Unguarded hour' (verse 6) I owe to Charlotte Elliott's hymn 'Christian, seek not yet repose'. In the final verse a reference to the past (line 2) is added to the present tense, and to the future reference ('for ever', BCP).

AT THE THRONE OF GRACE   55 88 55

Theme	Praise and worship
Written	at Ford, May 2004
Suggested tune	BOW CHURCH by Gerald Bullivant
	SEELENBRÄUTIGAM (or ARNSTADT, SPIRE, THURINGIA) attributed to Adam Drese

The text was written to the tune above, very familiar when sung to 'Round me falls the night' and perhaps less so to Basil Bridge's wedding hymn, 'Jesus, Lord, we pray'. The melody itself seems to go back for some 300 years, though its use as a hymn tune to a text in English is not known to me before the *English Hymnal* of 1906.

The subtitle, 'before worship' explains the purpose of the text; and it contains references to those main elements of public worship set out in the *Book of Common Prayer* at the Exhortation which begins the Order of Morning or Evening Prayer:

> And although we ought at all times humbly to acknowledge our sins before God; yet ought we most chiefly so to do, when we assemble and meet together to render thanks for the great benefits that we have received at his hands, to set forth his most worthy praise, to hear his most holy Word, and to ask those things which are requisite and necessary, as well for the body as the soul. Wherefore I pray and beseech you, as many as are here present, to accompany me with a pure heart, and humble voice, unto the throne of the heavenly grace, saying after me...

As will be seen, the thought of the 'throne of grace' (Hebrews 4.16), which concludes the Exhortation, both begins and ends the hymn. Within these references will be found Confession (verse 1, forgiveness, verse 2, pardon); Thanksgiving (verse 3); Praise (verse 3, worship); Scripture (verse 2); Intercession and Prayer (verse 3). The central couplet of verse 3 looks to the General Thanksgiving in the *Book of Common Prayer*, which speaks of showing God's praise 'not only with our lips, but in our lives'.

Theme	Mission and the Christian mind
Written	at Ford, July 2004
Suggested tune	DIES DOMINICA by J. B. Dykes
	EWING by Alexander Ewing
	MORNING LIGHT by G. J. Webb
	WOLVERCOTE by W. H. Ferguson

In Spring 2004 Samford University, of Birmingham, Alabama, announced a search for new hymn texts on the theme of 'Vocation, Faith and Learning', which would reflect the university's commitment to 'exemplify the faith journey from critical, theological reflection on mission to compassionate and liberating service in the world'. This text was written in response, though it did not prove to be what the University was seeking.

Verse 1 reminds us that 'in Christ' are 'hidden all the treasures of wisdom and knowledge', Colossians 2.3; and the Scriptures, rather than unaided reason or our own spiritual experience, offer us truth to live by. Verse 2 speaks of a needy world and the 'God-shaped void' of many hearts shown in our generation's hunger for the transcendent; together with the call for Christian thinkers to maintain and expound a world-view which begins with God as Creator. Verse 3 speaks of the call to commend Christ and his gospel in ways and words which resonate with the thinking of the day, and so offer hope to a materialistic and unbelieving society; while verse 4 is a prayer that God will use his people, and their gifts of mind and intellect, in the service of his Name and gospel, to bring the light and life of Christ to those who share our world.

BREAK INTO GLAD EXULTANT SONG   86 86 (CM)

Based on	Zephaniah 3.12–20
Theme	Rejoicing; redemption; restoration
Written	at Ford, July 2003
Suggested tune	ST BERNARD (German traditional)
	ST MAGNUS attributed to Jeremiah Clark
	ST STEPHEN by William Jones
	TIVERTON by Jacob Grigg

For a general explanation of this and other texts based on the minor prophets, see the Foreword and the Note on 'A righteous God in heaven reigns'.

This text looks to the concluding words of the Book of Zephaniah, the first of a new and long line of prophecy, often apocalyptic in form. The major part of Zephaniah's prophecy is judgment, even denunciation, from which it would be difficult to derive a hymn for Christian congregational worship. The final section, however is a wonderfully triumphant paean of praise to a God who restores because he loves.

The text draws on a number of translations. The opening words come straight from Knox, but RSV, REB, NIV and others play their part, sometimes supplying a single word. My first attempt was to a more ambitious metre, but this proved to be a cul-de-sac; and eventually the text seemed to fall most naturally into CM. Contrasts are drawn between our exultant song, and the Lord exulting over his people; and between the Lord's Name, as what we glory in (verse 3) and receive glory from (verse 5). 'Dust' is meant to carry overtones of our creation from the dust of the ground, to which we shall return (Genesis 2.7; 3.19): while (Ecclesiastes 12.7) the spirit returns to God. 'The ransomed of the Lord' (Isaiah 35.10) is a description of God's people which from its context is redolent of rejoicing, restoration and praise. 'Home' (verse 5) is from RSV, NRSV, NEB and NIV (Zephaniah 3.20).

The various shifts from the objective or general, to the first person plural, are a device to enable the singer to own and claim the blessings described, but with some proper self-effacement. So in verse 3, the final three lines talk of 'us' and 'our'; in verse 4 it is the final two lines; and in the final verse the personal claim is reserved for the concluding line, by way of climax, as much as to say 'All this that we have been rehearsing in terms of God's people belongs to us also, if we belong to him.'

CHRIST POURS HIS GRACE UPON HIS OWN   888 10 10

Theme	Grace; growth in Christ; unity
Written	at Ford, October 2004
Suggested tune	BESLAN by Ian Kellam
Published in	*Sing Praise to God: the hymn tunes of Ian Kellam* (USA), 2005 to BESLAN

When the composer Ian Kellam was at work on a large-scale score for the Royal Shakespeare Company's production of T. S. Eliot's *Murder in the Cathedral*, he included a setting of some medieval words, sung as a hymn:

> Out of this chaff was poured this corn
> And else the Church had been forlorn
> To Goddës grange now were thou born,
> O martyr Thoma, O martyr Thoma,
> O martyr Thoma, O martyr Thoma

In a letter of September 2004 Ian Kellam asked if I would write some contemporary words to his hymn tune, which he called BESLAN, in memory of the schoolchildren of Beslan killed in an act of terrorism not long before. He sent me the tune on a cassette, sung to the words set out above. The key seemed to me to lie in the final couplet. Since it was unlikely that this should again be an identical phrase repeated four times over in each verse, as in this lament, I experimented with rhyming couplets, but decided that 'to him [God] be glory' was a suitable conclusion to each verse, and that in consequence rhyme would find its place in the trio of opening lines, setting out some part of our faith which evokes the response 'to God be glory'. The shape of the short hymn is based on 'the Grace' (cf. 2 Corinthians 13.14), so that the theme of grace marks the whole text (in verse 2, as 'changeless love'), and it assumes a Trinitarian form, following the order used by the Apostle in his benediction.

Sing Praise to God, containing 18 of Ian Kellam's hymn tunes, is published by MorningStar Music Publishers, Fenton, Missouri, 63026–2024, USA.

GIVE THANKS TO GOD ABOVE   66 86 (SM)

Based on	Psalm 107
Theme	The love of God; God our strength
Written	at Ford, July 2004
Suggested tune	CARLISLE by Charles Lockhart
	DONCASTER by Samuel Wesley
	SANDYS (English traditional)
	SUNDERLAND by Henry Smart
	VENICE by William Amps

Reading this psalm one morning, with the aid of Derek Kidner's *Psalms 73–150* (London, 1975) I was struck with the four word-pictures which form the heart of the psalm, identified in the RSV by the introductory 'Some wandered...sat...were...went.' This is a division less obvious in the older translations, and Kidner describes the four scenes as likely to represent four ways of looking at the same reality. I have tried to follow this, but to use the verse divisions and the introductory 'In' to distinguish the four sections. The last line of my verse 2, with its echo of John 14.6, reminds the singer that he is no longer an ancient Israelite, but a follower of the risen and ascended Jesus; just as verse 4 looks to the Lord's words in Matthew 11.28.

My notebook, when wondering how best to approach a metrical version 'based on' this psalm, listed a number of alternative metres including 'possibly (?)' SM. In fact the lines seemed to fall naturally into this framework, thus avoiding a hymn of the length which six sections (prologue, the four word pictures and a conclusion) would require in a more spacious metre.

GLORY TO GOD, AND PRAISE   66 86 D (DSM)

Theme	Anniversary; praise and worship; the Holy Trinity; work
Written	at Ford, January 2005
Suggested tune	DIADEMATA by G. J. Elvey

In the summer of 2004 Professor John Salter, Chairman of the Tercentenary Celebration Committee of the Worshipful Company of Fan Makers (one of the ancient Livery Companies of the City of London), asked me if I might write the words of an anthem to mark their Tercentenary, suitable for congregational singing thereafter. He provided me with information about the Company, which received its royal charter from Queen Anne in 1709, and is active today in matters to do with education, the environment, and the City; with the history of their craft of ladies' fan making; and with modern developments of it in aeronautics, engineering, air-conditioning, ventilation and aspects of the work of the armed forces. It includes among its Statement of Aims a concern to 'play our part in the spiritual life of the City of London'.

If the text were to be suitable for congregational singing in the context of worship, it would need to be in the form of a hymn, though an anthem-setting might introduce variety of musical treatment. The text is Trinitarian; with creation and providence in verse 1; incarnation and redemption in verse 2 (line 3 offers a deliberate double meaning); and an invocation of the Spirit in verse 3. As seems fitting for a text written for an anniversary, verse 1 includes a glance backwards to the past; and the concluding verse looks forward to an eternal future.

There are a number of echoes or 'borrowings'. 'Ancient of Days' is a term from the Book of Daniel for the vision of God (7.9, 13, 22) and used with effect by earlier hymn writers; for example by Sir Robert Grant in 'O worship the King', first published in the 1830s. 'By wood and nails' is borrowed from a familiar prayer dating back to World War 1, 'O Jesus, Master Carpenter of Nazareth' (see Frank Colquhoun, *Prayers That Live*, London, 1981, page 38). 'The sum of things'—a phrase I have used before—comes to my mind from A. E. Housman's 'Epitaph on an army of mercenaries' (*Last Poems*, No. XXXVII), though its use can be traced back through Milton (for example) to classical sources: in the RSV translation it is used by Qoheleth, 'the Preacher' (Ecclesiastes 7.25). 'Shadows fade and flee' looks to the Song of Solomon (2.17), made familiar by Henry Lyte in 'Abide with me'; and perhaps by J. G. Whittier's phrase, 'shadows fall apart', in the last of the seventeen verses of his 'My Psalm'.

'GLORY TO THE GOD OF HEAVEN'   887 D

Theme	Christmas and Epiphany
Written	at Ford, November 2002
Suggested tune	EVANGELISTS by J. S. Bach and others

Written for our family Christmas card, 2003, this text derived its shape, and so to some extent its content, from the tune EVANGELISTS (No. 300 in *Hymns Ancient and Modern New Standard*). That tune also appears in *Common Praise*, 2000 as No. 319 to H. C. A. Gaunt's 'Praise the Lord, rise up rejoicing'.

In verse 1 of my text, the angel's voice (singular) is a reference to Luke 2.10–12, which prefaces the angelic chorus paraphrased in the opening lines of the hymn. In verse 4 the reference is to the angelic host (plural).

I would have much liked to borrow Charles Wesley's line for my verse 1: 'Dear Desire of every nation'. But this is hardly true of our divided and pluralistic world now that Wesley's justification for it from Haggai 2.7 is no longer thought by modern translators to be the prophet's meaning. 'Beyond our telling', in verse 2, I take to be synonymous with 'beyond conceiving or describing'; and the plural of 'borrows' in line 4 (cf. Hebrews 2.14) removes any ambiguity from the inversion. Line 5 contains an echo of Isaiah 53 (AV); while 'tasting death' follows Hebrews 2.9. The final line of the hymn echoes the opening line of the *Gloria in Excelsis,* authorship and age unknown, but going back at least to the fourth century; and used, for example, towards the end of the Holy Communion Service in the *Book of Common Prayer.*

HALLOW THE FATHER'S NAME   66 86 D (DSM)

Theme	Anniversary; celebration; praise and worship; the Holy Trinity
Written	at Ford, April 2003
Suggested tune	DIADEMATA by G. J. Elvey

Christian theology is firmly Trinitarian; and the hymn takes that as its framework, looking also at past, present and future. Amid the ascriptions and celebration, the last four lines of verses 2 and 3 are in the form of prayers, the first in terms of our responsibility in evangelism, teaching and proclamation; the second referring to service in the community, whether local or worldwide, echoing Isaiah 61 and the needs of our neighbour in Matthew 25.37f.

A few familiar phrases can be identified. 'Hallow', the opening word, takes us at once to the Lord's Prayer in Matthew 6 and Luke 11. It is a stronger word than 'honour' (which is used by J. B. Phillips) and goes back at least to Tyndale's translation of 1534. With the exception of the *Jerusalem Bible* of 1966 ('be held holy') the word is retained by all the most familiar translations: AV, RV, RSV, NRSV, NEB, REB, NIV and the *English Standard Version* of 2001. It is used in the Lord's Prayer by all those liturgies which (like *Common Worship*, 2000) follow the International Consultation on English Texts; and is the familiar prayer of many centuries from the *Book of Common Prayer* of the Church of England.

Christ as 'the Servant' (verse 2) is familiar from Isaiah, from Matthew 12.18 (quoting Isaiah 42) and from Philippians 2.7. Jesus speaks of his own servant role in Luke 22.27 and dramatizes it before the Last Supper. 'Love and joy and peace' (verse 3) are the first of the fruit of Spirit from Galatians 5.22; and binding the broken heart and freeing the captives are from Isaiah 61.

The Doxology borrows from the Book of Revelation (e.g. 5.13) and because of the familiarity of the phrase from Handel's *Messiah,* I have retained the liturgical 'unto' rather than some such phrase as 'be his alone'. 'Trinity of love' is not, I think, a phrase I have used before (though William Whiting in his 'Eternal Father, strong to save' has 'O Trinity of love and power') but helps to form a celebratory climax, especially borne aloft on the tune DIADEMATA to which the hymn was written.

HOW DARK THE NIGHT OF CLOUD AND CARES   86 84

Based on	Psalm 3
Theme	Evening; confidence and peace
Written	at Ford, February 2003
Suggested tune	ST CUTHBERT by J. B. Dykes

When pursuing the thought of looking again at psalms which I had not yet tried to put into metre, I found myself reading Psalm 3 with Derek Kidner's commentary, and being newly struck by it. At the same time I had identified 86 84 (to ST CUTHBERT) as a metre not yet attempted.

This metrical version has something in common with 'Safe in the shadow of the Lord', which is based on Psalm 91. Derek Kidner entitles that psalm 'Under his wings'; and though Psalm 3 bears the title 'The Dark Hour', verses 3 and 4 are headed 'Divine Protection', verses 5 and 6 'Peace of Mind', and verses 7 and 8 'Victory and Blessing'.

The first verse of the text uses the metaphor of night, cloud and darkness, to convey the hostility and enmity personified in the psalm. The mocking doubts are the 'voices taunting me' of Knox; 'encircling' in verse 3 is borrowed from the *Jerusalem Bible,* 'his people' comes from the closing words of the psalm, together with the thought of blessing. Peace is part of that blessing, as evidenced in the expressions of confidence that precede it: the shield, the glory, the lifting up of the head, the prayer heard, and so the quietness of mind and heart expressed in sleep.

HOW HAPPY THOSE INDEED

6666 4444

Based on	Psalm 1
Theme	Christian experience and discipleship
Written	at Ford, August 2002
Suggested tune	CROFT'S 136TH by William Croft
	EASTVIEW by Vernon Lee
	ST GODRIC by J. B. Dykes
	ST JOHN (or ADORATION) from *The Parish Choir*, 1851
Published in	*Eight Hymns, set 2*, 2004 to STOKESAY by Maurice Bevan

In August 2002 I began looking at the list of hymn texts I had based on individual psalms, with a view to adding to them; I did not have to look far! Psalm 1 has been well served in these decades by Michael Baughen's 'Blessed is the man', and I had therefore passed it by, although that version, perhaps as much an early worship song as a hymn, now dates back over 30 years. In the end, I wrote three versions in different metres, of which this was the first. When I came to look through them to include one in this present collection, I took advice from friends. This proved to be far from unanimous; so I have omitted the version in CM, and here include both the others.

Isaac Watts begins his *Psalms of David*, 1719, with three metrical versions of this psalm, which introduces (perhaps was written to introduce?) the whole Psalter. Watts uses CM, SM, and LM; and two of his three texts refer to Christ by name, which emboldens me to do the same here. It is unfortunate that the word 'blessed' (especially as 'blessèd') no longer sits easily to my ear in the opening line of a contemporary hymn. Alan Richardson writes (in his *A Theological Word Book of the Bible,* London, 1950) 'In the bible blessing means primarily the active outgoing of the divine goodwill or grace which results in prosperity and happiness amongst men.' So, while 'How happy...' does not exhaust the Psalmist's meaning, it seems the best phrase for our present purpose (cf. Gelineau, 'Happy indeed is the man...').

For the publication *Eight Hymns, set 2* see the Foreword, page viii.

HOW HAPPY THOSE WHO WALK IN TRUTH

86 888

Based on	Psalm 1
Theme	Christian experience and discipleship
Written	at Ford, August 2002
Suggested tune	REVELATION by Noël Tredinnick
	WITHINGTON by John Barnard
Published in	*Eight Hymns, set 2*, 2004 to HIGHGATE by Maurice Bevan

This is the second of three metrical versions of Psalm 1: see Note above. The third is not included in this present collection.

I was not aware when writing the text that I had used this metre before, 30 years earlier, for the hymn 'He walks among the golden lamps' (No. 199 in A *House of Praise*). The tune REVELATION, listed above, was written to that text (which is based on

Revelation 1.12–18); while WITHINGTON is John Barnard's tune, originally to Paul Wigmore's text based on Psalm 15, 'Lord, who may dwell within your house'. REVELATION was published first in *Psalm Praise*, 1973 and can be found in, for example, *Hymns for Today's Church*, 1982; and in *Praise!*, 2000. WITHINGTON can be found in *Psalms for Today*, 1990.

The word 'mansions' in the final verse is borrowed from John 14.2 (AV and RV).

R. W. Burchfield in his 1998 revision of *Fowler's Modern English Usage* allows that the word *nor* 'is occasionally used when there is no negative present or implied in the first clause', and this is the construction I follow in verse 1.

For the publication *Eight Hymns, set 2*, see the Foreword, page viii.

IN THE STILLNESS, HARK   55 88 55

Theme	Christmas and Epiphany
Written	at Ford, October 2004
Suggested tune	BOW CHURCH by Gerald Bullivant
	SEELENBRÄUTIGAM (or ARNSTADT, SPIRE, THURINGIA) attributed to Adam Drese
	WESTRON WYNDE by William Llewellyn

For the tune SEELENBRÄUTIGAM, see the earlier Note on 'At the throne of grace', which was written in May 2004. A few months later it occurred to me that this might well make a suitable tune for a Christmas hymn or carol.

Verse 1 of the text is a straightforward rendering of Luke 2.13,14. Verse 2 moves in thought to the prologue of St John, including a reference to 1 John 1.1 in the closing lines—where 'we' must be taken to mean 'we humans'. The thought in line 4 is drawn from the many references to Christ as Light, even as God is Light (1 John 1.5); and also to Christ as the agent of creation (cf. John 1.3). Line 4 of verse 3 takes two of the 'titles' given to Jesus in the Bible (Matthew 11.19; Isaiah 53.3) while verse 4 adds a third, transforming Peter's dreadful paradox ('And killed the Prince of life…' Acts 3.15, AV) into an affirmation of resurrection (line 2) and ascension (line 4). The final line of the hymn takes us back to Luke 2.11: William Barclay comments (*Jesus as They Saw Him*, London, 1962) that in the New Testament there are well over fifty occasions when the titles 'Christ' and 'Lord' are used together.

It was a happy discovery that there should be an alternative tune in this unusual metre, WESTRON WYNDE, contributed in 1965 to the *Anglican Hymn Book* by William Llewellyn, and named after the house where he lived as Director of Music at Charterhouse.

The text was first used on our family Christmas card, 2005.

JESUS CHRIST IS BORN TODAY   77 77 77

Theme	Christmas and Epiphany
Written	at Ford, November 2003
Suggested tune	HEATHLANDS by Henry Smart
	LUCERNA LAUDONIAE by David Evans
	NORICUM by Frederic James

Twice I have attempted to follow the Psalmist in the use of acrostics (Psalm 25: 'All my soul to God I raise' and Psalm 34: 'All our days we will bless the Lord', Nos. 138 and 142 in *A House of Praise*). It seemed that something of the same *jeu d'esprit*, if that is not too trivial a word for it, might make a fitting form for a Christmas celebration. Many carols are, by long tradition, essentially light-hearted. The opening line presented certain problems as the basis of the acrostic: words of differing length meant that in the vertical line the words 'IS BORN' had to be run together, and the first and last verses needed to end with a line which was not part of the vertical sentence. The text shows how this works. 'Prince' is several times used in Scripture as a title for Jesus: notably in Isaiah 9.6 ('Prince of peace'), Acts 3.15 ('Prince of life'), and Revelation 1.5 ('Prince of the kings of the earth'): it is this last which justifies the epithet 'universal'. 'Judge of all the earth' is an echo of Genesis 18.25; but numerous Messianic prophecies refer to the coming Christ as judge; as does Paul in, e.g., 2 Timothy 4.1, and Peter in 1 Peter 4.5.

One might expect to find other hymns with this opening line, but I have not done so. It echoes, of course, 'Jesus Christ is risen today' from *Lyra Davidica;* and there is a text in *The Faber Book of Carols,* translated as 'Jesus Christ is born tonight'. Charles Wesley gives us 'Christ the Lord is risen today'; but I find nothing comparable for Christmas, and indeed it is surprising how seldom Charles Wesley seems to open a hymn with the words 'Jesus Christ', though very often with 'Jesus' or 'Jesu'.

The text was first used on our family Christmas card, 2004.

LIGHT OF THE WORLD, TRUE LIGHT DIVINE   4444 6 D or 886 D

Theme   Christmas and Epiphany; Christ our Light
Written   at Ford, January 2002
Suggested tune   GROSVENOR by Edward Harwood
                       HULL (American traditional)
                       MANNA by J. G. Schicht

In my notebook, this is marked as 'one of those texts which came unsought…' The starting point was John 8.12: 'I am the Light of the world'; with the final line of verse 1 looking back to Isaiah 9.2. Verse 2 combines Christ's words, 'I am the life' from John 11.25 and John 14.6 with John 6.51 ('my flesh for the life of the world').

The final verse adds the ascription of 'Lord' (in the opening line) and 'Love' (in the final line) to the 'Light' and 'Life' of the preceding verses.

NOT OURS TO KNOW THE REASONS   76 76 D

Based on   The Book of Haggai
Theme   Advent; dedication and renewal; praise and worship
Written   at Ford, April 2003
Suggested tune   AURELIA by S. S. Wesley
                       DIES DOMINICA by J. B. Dykes

EWING by Alexander Ewing
GOSTERWOOD (English traditional)
PENLAN by David Jenkins

For a general explanation about this and other texts based on the minor prophets, see the Foreword and the Note on 'A righteous God in heaven reigns'.

Haggai's prophecy is set in a day of small things—small harvests, meagre rewards, little blessing, a people preoccupied with their own domestic affairs. Perhaps some churches today may find the portrait all too recognizable. Into this situation comes the call to build the Temple of the Lord, and the promise that God will be with them (1.13) to stir up the spirit of both leaders and people (14). These are the themes of the first twelve lines of the hymn, whose opening is in the spirit of Deuteronomy 29.29. But if the Temple be rebuilt, to God's greater glory, then the promise is of blessing and of a house filled with prosperity and (AV) peace (2.7–10). So the end of the second verse of the hymn can be read as a metaphor for the Temple once again standing at the 'heart of hearts' of the people; or, in Christian terms, of God indwelling the hearts of believers through the Spirit, and so making them, in New Testament terms, the Temple of the Lord (1 Corinthians 3.16).

Haggai concludes his prophecy in Messianic hope. Zerubbabel represents the renewed election of the Davidic line; and the 'shaking' (2.6) referred to in the final verse of the hymn is echoed in, e.g., Matthew 24.29. The famous description of Haggai 2.7 'the Desire of all nations' is now seen as a mistranslation, but one where the phrase carries its own truth (regardless of the exact meaning here) enshrined for centuries in the AV translation, and very much part of our current hymnody (though nowadays with a lower-case d) in, for example Charles Wesley's 'Come, thou long-expected Jesus', or James Montgomery's 'Angels from the realms of glory'.

O GOD, FROM AGE TO AGE THE SAME   88 88 88

Based on	Habakkuk 3
Theme	God the Father; trust in God
Written	at Ford, December 2003
Suggested tune	ALDERSGATE STREET by E. F. Horner
	PATER OMNIUM by Henry J. E. Holmes
	ST MATTHIAS by W. H. Monk

For a general explanation of this and other texts based on the minor prophets, see the Foreword and the Note on 'A righteous God in heaven reigns'.

We know little about Habakkuk, not where he came from, his ancestry or his tribe. Like Job, he takes it upon himself to ask God hard questions, affronted by a sense of injustice that the living God should remain silent when his covenant is broken. Like Job, too, he finds no easy answers, but a promise of hope and judgment leading to this prayer of reverence and faith. His prophecy is remembered for some vivid phrases: 'in wrath remember mercy'; 'revive your work in the midst of the years'; and the climactic insight, looking ahead to the new covenant in Jesus, 'the righteous shall live by his faith'.

This text draws its theme from the prayer or prophecy (both words are used) of Habakkuk's concluding chapter, introduced by the cry of 'Revive your work' and the reminder—much shortened from the original—of God's power and glory seen in the natural world. Verse 3 of the hymn looks to the well-known conclusion of the chapter, an affirmation of a faith which is tried but undaunted by disaster. William Cowper paraphrased this (see the Foreword, page viii) in one of the most familiar of his Olney hymns, 'Sometimes a light surprises', in what J. R. Watson (*An Annotated Anthology of Hymns*, Oxford, 2002) calls 'charming and harmonious verse'. This present paraphrase is perhaps more sombre than Cowper's, but in that at least not less true to Habakkuk's mind. In the last verse of the hymn 'strength' is from 3.19, 'Saviour' from verse 18 (JB, GNB); 'Judge' looks back to verses 5–13 of the prophecy while 'friend' has connotations mainly from the New Testament: though God is described as the friend of both Abraham and Moses. 'Rejoice' and 'exult' come together in, for example, the REB verse 18. The concluding couplet looks to the Knox translation 'he will bring me safely on my way'.

O GOD OF PEACE, WHO GAVE US BREATH AND BIRTH 10 10 10 10 10 10

Theme	The peace of the world
Written	at Ford, December 2003
Suggested tune	UNDE ET MEMORES by W. H. Monk

In 2003 Macalester Plymouth United Church of St Paul, Minnesota, and the Presbytery of the Two Cities Area, let it be known that they were looking for new hymn texts, to a familiar metre, on the call of the church to work for peace; this was their eighth international contest for an English hymn. This text was written in response and proved to be the hymn they were seeking; it was first sung at morning worship on Sunday 23 May 2004.

A number of Bible passages can be recognized: 'God of peace' comes in at least four books of the New Testament; 'peace in (my) days' is used by Isaiah (39.8) as well as in Kings and Chronicles; 'Prince of peace' is from Isaiah 9.6; 'making peace' from Matthew 5.9; 'peace I leave with you' from John 14.27; the Spirit's fruit from Galatians 5.22; unity in 'the bond of peace' from Ephesians 4.3; 'peaceable wisdom' from James 3.17; the uplifted countenance (coupled with peace) from Numbers 6.26. One other 'borrowing' deserves mention: line 3 of the final verse is from President J. F. Kennedy's Inaugural Address of 20 January 1961 which spoke of 'a new world of law, where the strong are just and the weak secure and the peace preserved'. In the final verse the allusion is to the prophecy of Micah 4.3, 'Nation shall not lift up sword against nation', which continues 'neither shall they learn war any more'.

O GOD THE JUST, ENTHRONED ON HIGH 88 86

Based on	Malachi 3 & 4
Theme	Advent; God the Father; judgment; love of God
Written	at Ford, August 2002
Suggested tune	CHILDHOOD from *A Student's Hymnal*, 1923
	SAFFRON WALDEN by A. H. Brown

For a general explanation of this and other texts based on the minor prophets, see the Foreword and the Note on 'A righteous God in heaven reigns'.

Malachi is the final book of the Old Testament, and the voice of prophecy is then silent until the coming of John the Baptist. Chapter 2 ends with the question, 'Where is the God of justice?' and the final sections of the book respond with the promise that a messenger is on his way and that 'the Lord whom you seek will suddenly come…' It is on these two closing chapters that this text draws.

The original opening, 'O God of justice', gave place to the present line when it became clear that the break in the first line of each verse should come after four syllables, not five. God's balance—memorably part of Daniel's translation of the mysterious message on the wall of Belshazzar's palace (Daniel 5.27)—is an image borrowed from Isaiah (40.12); while the judgment seat is a New Testament phrase from Romans 14.10 and 2 Corinthians 5.10. The cry 'How long?' is echoed by the Psalmist and the prophets, and by the martyrs of Revelation 6.10.

'Who can stand?' (verse 3) is from Malachi 3.2 while 3.6,7 speak of the unchanging nature of God and of his readiness to stand by his covenant with Israel if they will return (see my verse 4). 'Sacrifice of praise' (a key concept of the Service of Holy Communion) is from Hebrews 13.15; while the phrase 'the windows of heaven' is one of the most familiar of Malachi's images (NEB, 'windows in the sky'; JB, 'floodgates of heaven'; Malachi 3.10). In the final verse of the text 'the Sun of Righteousness…with healing in his wings' is taken directly from Malachi 4.2.

Of the limited number of tunes, two include repetition, and the text is therefore designed so that the final couplet of each verse can be repeated.

Like most of its companions, this is not a metrical paraphrase of these two chapters of Malachi; but he provides much of the inspiration, and echoes of both his thought and his expression help to make a Christian hymn of praise, especially suitable for Advent.

O GOD, WHOSE THRONE ETERNAL STANDS   86 86 D (DCM)

Theme	Love of God; pilgrimage; praise and worship; saints
Written	at Ford, January 2005
Suggested tune	CLAUDIUS adapted from G. W. Fink
	LADYWELL by W. H. Ferguson
	PRECIOUS WORDS (composer unknown)
	SERAPH (or EVANGEL) by G. W. Fink
	ST MATTHEW by William Croft

Hymnody is often a means of celebrating, and reflecting on, the faithfulness of God. 'Great is thy faithfulness' surely owes to this some of its immense popularity. We meet the same thought in the closing verse (often the only verse now remembered) of Joseph Hart's hymn on Deuteronomy 13, 'No prophet, nor dreamer of dreams', where God is described as 'our faithful unchangeable friend'. This text is a celebration of that unchangeableness, experienced by us his children as 'faithfulness'.

Verse 1 contrasts the eternal reign of God with the 'passing years' and allotted span of us, his creatures. Against this background, and conscious of his mercies and faithfulness, we give ourselves to praise. Verse 2 continues this theme, looking back before our birth, and forward to the day when death is swallowed up in Christ's victory (1 Corinthians 15.54).

The second half of the verse draws deliberately on the Bidding Prayer before a Carol Service, published by Eric Milner-White in his *Daily Prayer* (Oxford, 1941) and used for many years by King's College, Cambridge in their Service of Lessons and Carols traditionally broadcast on Christmas Eve.

Verse 3 reminds us that praise on earth is part of the praise of heaven. Psalm 145.4 and Malachi 3.6 inform the thought of God's changelessness and our unity in Christ with the Church Triumphant. The second half of the verse brings in the heart of the gospel which we celebrate. The Holy Spirit was referred to in verse 2; here the reference to Christ (cf. Hebrews 13.8) makes the whole hymn Trinitarian. Finally in verse 4 we turn from the past and the present to the future, with joy and confidence rooted in God's fatherliness and faithfulness, ending with a reminder of what was declared in verse 3, that 'I am the Lord: I change not' (Malachi 3.6).

For the phrase 'a farther shore', see the Note on 'Almighty Father, God of grace' on page 42.

O SPIRIT OF THE SOVEREIGN LORD   86 86 (CM) *or*
                                                    86 86 D (DCM)

Based on	Isaiah 61.1–3
Theme	Church and congregation; ministry; new life in Christ
Written	at Ford, December 2002
Suggested tune	CM:
	BISHOPTHORPE by Jeremiah Clarke
	IRISH from *A Collection of Hymns and Sacred Poems*, 1749
	REDHEAD 66 (or METZLER) by Richard Redhead
	ST STEPHEN by William Jones
	DCM:
	CLAUDIUS adapted from G. W. Fink

Hearing Isaiah 66 read in our local church from the NIV gave me the opening line, and encouraged me to try to write a hymn based, however loosely, on this famous passage. Our Lord's own use of it at Nazareth (Luke 4.16f) not only indicates its Messianic nature, but justifies its use in the context of Christian ministry; so that I see this as a hymn with special reference to the ordination, licensing, commissioning or recognizing of people in some way set apart for ministry; whether it be at an ordination, a Diocesan Readers' Service, or a Service for the Sunday School teachers and other 'lay ministers' of a local church.

In verse 2, line 4, just as the 'want' that oppresses those in poverty may be none of their own making, so the 'sin' may be their own or (perhaps more likely) that of others, or of society. In verse 4, line 3, I have transmuted the prophet's 'day of vengeance' to something nearer the Knox translation which talks of the Lord who 'will give us redress'. The underlying thought is of God's justice and righteousness.

By the end of the hymn, what began with those 'set apart' very much in mind has become a prayer for the ministry of all God's people, embracing both the call to make known the gospel in teaching and proclamation, and the disciple's duty to be the salt and light and servant of the world in which God has placed us.

For myself, I prefer to see this as a DCM text of three verses, which is how it began. But DCM tunes are not easy to find; and some congregations may therefore prefer to sing it as six CM verses, for which of course there is a wide choice of tunes. A distinguished precedent for offering such a choice can be found in Charles Wesley's 'Love divine, all loves excelling'. It too was written in a double metre; but *Hymns Ancient and Modern* in 1889 and 1916 made it an 87 87 hymn of six verses (omitting the original verse 2). *Common Praise*, 2000 prints both versions of Charles Wesley's text, one as 87 87 and the other as 87 87 D.

OUR FATHER GOD WHO GAVE US BIRTH   88 88 88

Theme	Death and heaven; funeral
Written	at Ford, May 2004
Suggested tune	MELITA by William Whiting

In 1966 I was asked to write a hymn for Peter Thistlethwayte, as High Sheriff of Essex, Zto the tune MELITA for a Justice Service (see *A House of Praise*, No. 278 'O God, whose all-sustaining hand'). In August 2003 I received a further request on his behalf, this time for a funeral hymn which could be sung to the same tune, to file away against the day (still, we hoped, far in the future) when it might be needed. This is the origin of this text.

The hymn begins with the thought of God as our Creator and Sustainer, and ourselves as his loved and ransomed children for whom he gave his Son, as one who 'has borne our griefs and carried our sorrows' (Isaiah 53.4). Verse 2 looks back over an earthly life of faith, with joy triumphing over sorrow, with work fulfilled, blessings enjoyed, and love and life secure in the confidence of Christ's resurrection. The reference to sea and sky is a reminder that Peter Thistlethwayte is a sailor (hence his choice of tune), but praise for the world of nature, and for the experience of human love and affection is common to us all. Verse 3 is an affirmation of this living and personal faith, through the cross of Christ, and in his Person and word. The last two lines draw on John 10, especially verses 27 and 28. In verse 4 there is an echo of, e.g. 1 Kings 8.56 and of John 14.2,3.

PRINCE OF LIFE AND LORD OF GLORY   87 87 77

Theme	Ascension; the Lord Jesus Christ; Christian experience and discipleship
Written	at Ford, February 2005
Suggested tune	ALL SAINTS adapted by W. H. Monk
	NEANDER by Joachim Neander

The aim of this hymn is to offer a congregation words in which they can recall together the life of Christ on earth, and relate some aspects of it to their own experience. Over the centuries, many hymns have made the stories written in the Gospels their starting point. Charles Wesley gave us 'O Thou, whom once they flocked to hear'; John Newton, 'One there is above all other'; Horatius Bonar, 'I heard the voice of Jesus say'.

'Prince of life' in verse 1 is Peter's phrase, from his impromptu sermon in Solomon's porch (Acts 3.15, AV, JBP, JB). 'Lord of glory' is used by Paul (1 Corinthians 2.8) and James (2.1). I discovered during the writing of this text that there is an earlier hymn, 'Lord of life and King of glory' by Christian Burke (d. 1944); but it is specifically on the theme of motherhood, in a slightly different metre, and seems now to have fallen out of use. Before I knew this, I had considered what would have been an identical first line; but in fact am better pleased with the opening: 'Prince of life…'

Verse 2 has in mind passages such as Luke 4.22 and John 7.46; 'love divine' in verse 3 is an echo of Charles Wesley, and in verse 4 '…remember me' is meant to bring to mind the thief on the cross. In the final verse the title 'Prince of life', originally in the sombre context of 'And killed the Prince of life', here reminds the worshipper that Peter went on to add 'But God raised him from the dead' (NEB). This triumphant vindication, with the finishing of Christ's work and the resurrection with him of the believer, concludes the hymn on a note of affirmation and joy.

TEACH US YOUR VOICE TO HEAR 66 86 (SM)

Based on	Mark 12.29–31
Theme	Love for God
Written	at Ford, August 2002
Suggested tune	FRANCONIA by W. H. Havergal
	ST THOMAS (Williams) by Aaron Williams
	SOUTHWELL from William Damon's *Psalmes*, 1579
	VENICE by William Amps

This short text arises from hearing as a Gospel reading in our local church the reply of Jesus to 'one of the scribes' as to which is the great commandment. I had originally supposed that a hymn of four verses might take a different word for each: perhaps 'heart', 'soul', 'mind', and 'strength'. But this is the form in which it eventually came, with these four words (from, e.g., Mark 12.30, building on Deuteronomy 6.5) concluding the second verse.

In verse 1, 'godly fear' is from Hebrews 12.28 (JBP has 'holy fear'). The opening line of verse 2 is from the RSV translation of the first verse of 1 Corinthians 14: 'Make love your aim.' In the last stanza the phrase 'who loved us first' is taken from 1 John 4.19 in NEB, NRSV and other more modern translations: 'We love because he loved us first.' There is no comma at the end of that line, to indicate that it is primarily God's love, more than our own, which never ends. Paul in 1 Corinthians 13.8 (RSV) makes this a statement about the very nature of love, and in that sense it may be appropriate that there is this unresolved ambiguity in my closing line.

THE FINAL TRIUMPH WON 66 66 88

Theme	Eastertide; rejoicing; resurrection
Written	at Ford, December 2002
Suggested tune	MILLENNIUM (source unknown)
Published in	*Christian Hymns*, 2004 to MILLENNIUM

In December 2002 our family Christmas card carried the text 'The light of glory breaks', for which I had discovered the tune MILLENNIUM, believed to be English in origin, but first published by Henry Ward Beecher in an American collection of 1855. It was running in my head, and seemed appropriate for Easter as much as for Christmas.

The verses speak in turn of the achievement of the cross, sealed by the resurrection of Christ; of the historic facts of Christ's resurrection, ascension and exaltation; and of ourselves as 'risen with Christ'. Bible references include Colossians 2.15 ('his final glorious triumphant act' JBP); Romans 5.11; Philippians 2.12,13; Ephesians 1.4; 1 Peter 1.18; 1 Corinthians 15.55; Philippians 2.9; Hebrews 1.3; Colossians 3.1.

Verse 1 is therefore rooted in eternity, verse 2 in history; verse 3 is a bridge between the historical and the eternal, and verse 4 between the objective and the subjective: the facts of our faith, and our experience. The final line of each verse repeats the essential message of resurrection and relates it to light out of darkness, life out of death, the cross before the crown, and his people's united praise for the Christ who gives himself to us.

THE GOD OF WHOM THE PROPHETS TOLD   88 88 (LM)

Based on	The Book of Zechariah
Theme	Advent; grace; the love of God; the Lord Jesus Christ
Written	at Ford, December 2002
Suggested tune	CHURCH TRIUMPHANT by J. W. Elliott
	EISENACH by J. H. Schein
	HAWKHURST by H. J. Gauntlett
	HERONGATE (English traditional)
	IVYHATCH by Bertram Luard-Selby
	SOLOTHURN (Swiss traditional)

For a general explanation of this and other texts based on the minor prophets, see the Foreword and the Note on 'A righteous God in heaven reigns'.

The hymn is not a paraphrase of any one part of Zechariah, still less an exposition of his prophecy, but simply a borrowing of his images, especially where they carry for the Christian reader a Messianic interpretation. Most of us would agree with the idea that 'the human mind is not a debating hall, but a picture gallery', or, as C. S. Lewis put it 'Reason is the natural organ of truth; but imagination is the organ of meaning' (*Selected Literary Essays*, Cambridge, 1969, page 265). *'Image'*, in Zechariah as elsewhere, appeals therefore directly to the *imagination*. It is possible, with a generous interpretation, to put chapter and verse beside each line of the hymn.

Zechariah has other pictures I should have liked to include; for example the man with the measuring line (who appeared in a first draft but was later omitted); the delightful and well-known description of Zion in 8.4,5; the ten men clutching a Jew's robe (8.23), and the evocative 'prisoners of hope' (9.12). But five stanzas is surely enough for a hymn of this nature: Charles Wesley chose to expound the armour of God in 16 verses (128 lines) of 'Soldiers of Christ, arise', but his brother in the famous *Collection* of 1780 made of this three hymns for congregational singing, each of 32 lines, and still had four verses left over. I think the moral, as far as hymnody is concerned, is that enough is enough!

THE PROMISED LIGHT OF ALL THE EARTH 86 86 (CM)

Based on   Luke 2.22–38
Theme   The Presentation of Christ in the Temple; Christ our Light
Written   at Ford, February 2003
Suggested tune   CM
                    ABRIDGE (or ST STEPHEN) by Isaac Smith
                    ARDEN by George Thalben-Ball
                    JACKSON (or BYZANTIUM) by Thomas Jackson
                    ST TIMOTHY by H. W. Baker
                    STOCKTON by Thomas Wright

In the present liturgical calendar of the Church of England, 'the Presentation of Christ in
the Temple' falls on 2 February, forty days after Christmas. There is a reference to its
observance at Jerusalem in the fourth century, and from the sixth century the Eastern
Christian tradition was to call it simply 'the Meeting' (of Christ with Simeon and Anna).
A reference to 'meeting' is included in the last verse of this text.

The 'Light' of the first line is from Simeon's song, our *Nunc Dimittis* of Luke 2.32.
Stanza 3 takes up Simeon's prophecy to Mary (verses 34,35) in the fuller light of the
gospel; and this leads to the testimony and thankfulness of stanza 4 (cf. verse 38).

The thought of the presentation of Christ becomes, in stanza 5, the presentation of ourselves; and the sacrifice offered by Mary and Joseph (verse 24) is suggested by our sacrifice of praise, in deed as well as word. The final stanza links the 'meeting' of Christ in the
Temple with his risen presence and our contemporary meeting with him; whether in a
first encounter or in the daily discipleship whose fruits (lines 3 and 4) may bring to mind
our Lord's own growth to maturity in the final verse of Luke 2.

The pre-Reformation name 'Candlemas' was reintroduced into the Church of England
liturgy in *Common Worship*, 2000; the use of lights on that day is perhaps derived in part
from Luke 2.32. The name (in Old English) goes back to at least the eleventh century.

THOUGH ONE WITH GOD IN FORM DIVINE 88 88 (LM)

Based on   Philippians 2.6–11
Theme   Passiontide; the Lord Jesus Christ
Written   at Ford, August 2002
Suggested tune   BOW BRICKHILL by S. H. Nicholson
                    FULDA by William Gardiner
                    RIMINGTON by Francis Duckworth
                    WAREHAM by William Knapp

These six verses of Philippians 2 have been described as 'a purple patch' within the fabric
of Paul's urgent exhortation, and have long been regarded as a quotation, possibly of a
hymn. Various attempts have been made to show their symmetry and to print them as
stanzas, and many hymn writers have drawn inspiration from them. Think, for example,

of Caroline Noel's 'At the name of Jesus' or F. Bland Tucker's 'All praise to thee…' or Charles Wesley's 'Arise my soul, arise'.

In this metrical paraphrase 'form' in the opening line follows the AV and most modern translations, though NIV and Knox have 'nature'. 'Self-surrender' and 'stripped himself' express the literal 'emptied himself' of RV and RSV, equivalent to the 'made himself nothing' of NIV or the 'dispossessed himself' of Knox. 'Obedient' (stanza 3) appears in almost all translations, and 'exaltation' in AV, NIV, NRSV, REB and others.

Stanzas 6 and 7 stress the New Testament affirmation that it is God the Father who exalts his Son, and who bestows on him the Name, and it is to God's glory that we confess and worship him. Singers are reminded that the text moves from willing self-surrender and obedience to the cross, to exaltation and praise, and in the final line to triumphant affirmation. These differing moods need to be reflected in our song.

THROUGH STORMY CLOUD AND DARKNESS DEEP   88 88 88

Based on	Ezekiel 34; John 10; 1 Peter 5
Theme	Christ the Shepherd; growth in Christ, ministry
Written	at Ford, November 2002
Suggested tune	ST MATTHIAS (Monk) by W. H. Monk

The text was written in response to a request, circulated through the Hymn Society in the United States and Canada, for a hymn to support a Worship and Christian Education event: 'Tools for the Journey: Equipping the Saints', in March 2003. The event was sponsored by the Lower Susquehanna Synod of the Evangelical Lutheran Church in America, and this was chosen as the Hymn of the Day for the opening service on 1 March 2003. From the passages of Scripture suggested by the Synod organizers (see 'Based on…' above, with the addition of John 10) the text takes the thought of God as the Shepherd of (the new) Israel, Christ as the Good Shepherd, and the elders or ministers of his church as under-shepherds; with the thought of seeking the lost and the nurture, growth and protection of the flock, leading at last to glory.

Stanza 1 of my text draws on Ezekiel 34.12, 'a day of clouds and thick darkness', while 'one flock, one Shepherd' is from John 10.16. The 'new shepherds' of my stanza 3 has in mind Paul's farewell to the Ephesian elders (Acts 20.28, where the NEB uses the phrase 'shepherds of the church'), and Peter's charge to the elders (1 Peter 5.1,2, where again the NEB translates 'taking the oversight' as 'whose shepherds you are'.) The last lines of the hymn refer to Revelation 7.9 and to 1 Corinthians 13.12.

TO GOD BE GLORY, LOVE AND PRAISE   886 D

Based on	Luke 8.2,3; John 19.25; 20.11f
Theme	Mary Magdalene; forgiveness; love for God
Written	at Ford, November 2002
Suggested tune	CORNWALL by S. S. Wesley
	MANNA by J. G. Schicht

In November 2002 the vicar of St Mary Magdalene, Norwich (a church I knew well from my time in the diocese), wrote to tell me of their forthcoming centenary. St Mary's is known for its openness to the community (symbolized by a vast clear glass window at the west end, so that passers-by see into the building) and for its caring and reconciling ministry.

This text therefore begins with the church, looking back (over the hundred years of its life) and speaking of its welcome for all. Mary herself, and the themes of forgiveness and acceptance are introduced in verse 2; which relates to the account in Luke 8 of her deliverance and healing and how she accompanied Jesus in his ministry thereafter. Verse 3 comes to the heart of our own deliverance, the love that comes from sins forgiven; and the accounts in Matthew, Mark and John of Mary among the women who stood by the cross 'afar off', and heard the witness of the centurion. Verse 4 reminds us of Mary at the grave of Jesus, and of how the risen Christ (whom she mistook for Joseph's gardener) appeared and spoke to her on Easter morning.

These great central facts of the Gospel story are related to the present through what the church of St Mary Magdalene stands for today; and in the final verses by the prayer that we may share Mary's experience ourselves.

Verse 3 contains three uses of the word 'love': our love, Christ's love; and Christ who is love. Line 3 is drawn from John 15.9,10; line 4 from Philippians 3.8. 'Endless life' in verse 4 is from Hebrews 7.16. The final line of verse 3 must owe something to a memory of the longer line 'My Lord, my Love is crucified', which was used both by Charles Wesley in 'O Love divine, what has thou done?' and in John Wesley's translation, 'O Lord, enlarge our scanty thought'. There is a valuable discussion of the original source from St Ignatius in Richard Watson and Kenneth Trickett, *Companion to Hymns & Psalms* (Peterborough, 1988) under hymns 175 and 568.

The tune MANNA comes from 19th-century Germany and is unrelated to the American tune of the same period, HOLY MANNA (87 87 D), compiled by William Moore.

Mary Magdalene is traditionally commemorated on 22 July, for which the Church of England *Common Worship* provides alternative collects and a post-communion prayer.

TO GOD MOST HIGH BE GIVEN   76 76 D

Based on	The opening Exhortations at Morning and Evening Prayer, BCP, ASB, *Common Worship*
Theme	Praise and worship
Written	at Ford, February 2004
Suggested tune	AURELIA by S. S. Wesley
	DIES DOMINICA by J. B. Dykes
	EWING by Alexander Ewing
	MORNING LIGHT by G. J. Webb

This is a hymn designed to echo the opening Exhortations of morning or evening worship, whether by supplementing them, or perhaps by taking their place in a less formal Service. The structure, whether in the *Book of Common Prayer*, the Deposited Book of 1928, the *Alternative Service Book*, 1980, or in *Common Worship* is not dissimilar. Each contains elements preparing us for worship, praise and thanksgiving; for confession and penitence; for the careful hearing of Scripture; and for prayer and intercession for ourselves and others. These will be immediately recognizable in the hymn, sometimes in the exact phrases of one or other of the Exhortations.

The phrase 'common supplication' may remind some of the Prayer of St Chrysostom which serves to conclude Morning or Evening Prayer; and 'thankfulness unmeasured' is akin to the 'inestimable' or 'immeasurable' of the General Thanksgiving. 'Sacrifice of praise' is from, for example, Hebrews 13.15; and is a phrase of special significance where it appears in the first post-communion thanksgiving of the *Book of Common Prayer*. 'The service of our days' takes up the thought found most explicitly in the *Common Worship* exhortation, 'that by the power of the Holy Spirit we may give ourselves to the service of God'.

TO JOSEPH OF NAZARETH GOD GAVE INTEGRITY   13 10 13 10

Theme	Joseph of Nazareth; family; work
Written	at Ford, November 2003
Suggested tune	WAS LEBET, WAS SCHWEBET
	from J. H. Rheinhardt's *Choralbuch*, 1754

Joseph's name does not figure largely in the Gospel record: the only references to him by name are in the accounts of the nativity given by Matthew, and in Luke 4.22. But Joseph was surely still living and active when Jesus was twelve years old (Luke 2.41f) even if the references to him in Luke 4.22 and Matthew 13.55, near the start of Jesus' public ministry, do not show conclusively whether he was then alive. But to have been chosen as foster-father to Jesus, even if only through his early years (supposing, as some legends suggest, that Joseph died young), implies unimaginable honour. 'Integrity' in my verse 1 is meant as a reminder of this, as evidenced by Joseph's concern to preserve Mary's reputation (Matthew 1.19).

Perhaps because of an unbiblical devotion to, or cult of, Joseph in other parts of the Christian church from about the fifth century, and perhaps because he was cast as a figure of 'comic relief' in some medieval mystery plays, Joseph's name did not appear in the Anglican Prayer Books or Calendars of 1549, 1552 or 1662. The *Alternative Service Book,* 1980 (following long Roman Catholic tradition) designated 19 March to be his Festival and included a simple collect composed by the Liturgical Commission. This innovation *Common Worship* has continued (page 428), elaborating the collect (and adding a version of it in Elizabethan language, page 501) as well as providing a newly-written post-communion prayer.

The text took shape at first in the unusual metre of 6 6 10 D, with the opening line simply as 'Joseph of Nazareth'. But musical friends advised me that there was no existing tune which accurately fitted such a text, and with their encouragement I worked instead to the tune WAS LEBET, WAS SCHWEBET, well-known when sung to J. S. B. Monsell's 'O worship the King'.

'Strengthener' in the final verse caused me much thought. Possible alternatives would be 'Comforter', as in the AV, but the meaning of the word is now almost entirely that of consolation rather than strength. 'Advocate' is less happy metrically, and carries the same objection as the NIV 'Counsellor'. Indeed 'Counsellor' is really US usage in this context. 'Advocate' in a Trinitarian setting suffers too from the use in 1 John 2.1 where our primary Advocate is Christ. I was encouraged by the fact that the etymology of 'Comforter' is from 'strengthen'; and by the thought that not every title can exhaust the attributes of the Person named. God is not only Father; Christ is other things besides Saviour (e.g. Intercessor); and there seems no reason why we should not use the title 'Strengthener' (cf. Ephesians 3.16) even if it does not exhaust the Spirit's work.

Besides the Festival of Joseph of Nazareth in March, the hymn would also be suitable in the celebration of home and family life, or of daily work; or as part of Christmas worship.

WHAT SENSE OF NEED LED ANDREW ON   88 88 (LM) *or*
                                                          88 88 D (DLM)

Theme	St Andrew; call of God; mission
Written	at Ford, November 2003
Suggested tune	DLM:
	LONDON (ADDISON'S) by John Sheeles
	RADIANT CITY by Thomas Pavlechko
	LM:
	HERONGATE (English traditional)
	MORNING HYMN by François H. Barthélémon
	WAREHAM by William Knapp

Andrew, like his brother Peter, was a fisherman. His name means 'manly', so perhaps, like Peter, he too could be called 'the big fisherman'. Mark 1.29 tells us they shared a house at Capernaum, on the northern shore of the Sea of Galilee, though (John 1.44) natives of Bethsaida. Verse 1 of this text draws on John's account of Andrew with John the Baptist (John 1.35f); while the second half of verse 2 refers to the calling of Andrew in e.g. Mark 1.16–18.

Andrew is mentioned by name in John's account of the feeding of the five thousand (John 6.8); but it is the finding of Peter, and the pointing of the Greeks to Christ (John 12.20–22) which have made him, as 'the first missionary', associated with mission and evangelism. In the Church of England his Festival is kept on 30 November, with a collect in the *Book of Common Prayer* taken from the 1552 book, and included largely unchanged in *Common Worship* among the 'traditional' collects (page 516). St Andrew's Eve, 29 November, is set aside as a day of Intercession and Thanksgiving for the Missionary Work of the Church; and this important aspect of Andrew's commemoration is reflected in verse 2 and especially in the closing lines of verse 3, of this text.

The tune RADIANT CITY is better known in the United States than in the United Kingdom, but can be found (no doubt among other places) in *Praise!*, 2000.

INDEXES

Index of Biblical References

Please see the Foreword for further details

Themes from the Liturgical Calendar

*See the Index of Themes and Subjects, page 73, for Advent,
Christmas and Epiphany, Passiontide, Eastertide, Ascension, Trinity*

* *The Presentation of Christ in the Temple,* 2 February
  The promised Light of all the earth

* *Joseph of Nazareth,* 19 March
  To Joseph of Nazareth God gave integrity

* *Mary Magdalene,* 22 July
  To God be glory, love and praise

  Bible Sunday
  To God Most High be given

  Remembrance Sunday
  O God of peace, who gave us breath and birth

* *St Andrew,* 30 November
  What sense of need led Andrew on

* not found in the Index of Themes and Subjects in *A House of Praise*
  which otherwise contains many hymns for the days and seasons of the
  Christian year

Metrical Index

4444 6 D
Light of the world, true light divine

55 88 55
At the throne of grace
In the stillness, hark

6666 4444
Angelic hosts above
How happy those indeed

66 66 88
The final triumph won

66 86 (SM)
Give thanks to God above
Teach us your voice to hear

66 86 D (DSM)
Glory to God, and praise
Hallow the Father's Name

76 76 D
Beyond what mind can measure
Not ours to know the reasons
To God Most High be given

77 77 77
Jesus Christ is born today

86 84
How dark the night of cloud and cares

86 86 (CM)
Break into glad exultant song
O Spirit of the Sovereign Lord
The promised Light of all the earth

86 86 D (DCM)
O God, whose throne eternal stands
O Spirit of the Sovereign Lord

86 888
How happy those who walk in truth

87 87 77
Prince of life and Lord of glory

884
As Jesus taught us, first we pray

886 D
Light of the world, true light divine
To God be glory, love and praise

887 D
'Glory to the God of heaven'

88 86
O God the Just, enthroned on high

88 88 (LM)
A righteous God in heaven reigns
The God of whom the prophets told
Though one with God in form divine
What sense of need led Andrew on

88 888 (LM extended)
A righteous God in heaven reigns

88 88 88
O God, from age to age the same
Our Father God who gave us birth
Through stormy cloud and darkness deep

88 88 D (DLM)
Almighty Father, God of grace
What sense of need led Andrew on

888 10 10
Christ pours his grace upon his own

10 10 10 10 10 10
O God of peace, who gave us breath and
 birth

13 10 13 10
To Joseph of Nazareth God gave integrity

Index of Suggested Tunes

ST DROSTANE
A righteous God in heaven reigns

ST GODRIC
How happy those indeed

ST JOHN (*or* ADORATION)
How happy those indeed

ST MAGNUS (Clark)
Break into glad exultant song

ST MATTHEW
O God, whose throne eternal stands

ST MATTHIAS (Monk)
O God, from age to age the same
Through stormy cloud and darkness deep

ST STEPHEN (Jones)
Break into glad exultant song
O Spirit of the Sovereign Lord
The promised Light of all the earth

ST THOMAS (Williams)
Teach us your voice to hear

ST TIMOTHY
The promised Light of all the earth

THURINGIA (*or* SEELENBRÄUTIGAM)
At the throne of grace
In the stillness, hark

TIVERTON
Break into glad exultant song

TORQUAY
A righteous God in heaven reigns

UNDE ET MEMORES
O God of peace, who gave us breath and birth

VENICE
Give thanks to God above
Teach us your voice to hear

WAREHAM
Though one with God in form divine
What sense of need led Andrew on

WAS LEBET, WAS SCHWEBET
To Jesus of Nazareth God gave integrity

WESTRON WYNDE
In the stillness, hark

WINCHESTER NEW
A righteous God in heaven reigns

WITHINGTON
How happy those who walk in truth

WOLVERCOTE
Beyond what mind can measure

Index of Themes and Subjects

Pilgrimage
  O God, from age to age the same
  O God, whose throne eternal stands
Praise and worship
  Angelic hosts above
  At the throne of grace
  Glory to God, and praise
  Hallow the Father's Name
  Not ours to know the reasons
  O God, whose throne eternal stands
  To God Most High be given
Prayer
  As Jesus taught us, first we pray
  To God Most High be given
Presentation of Christ in the Temple
  Light of the world, true light divine
  The promised Light of all the earth
Redemption
  Break into glad exultant song
  Glory to God, and praise
  Light of the world, true light divine
  The final triumph won
  Though one with God in form divine
Rejoicing
  Almighty Father, God of grace
  Break into glad exultant song
  Give thanks to God above
  'Glory to the God of heaven'
  O God the Just, enthroned on high
  Not ours to know the reasons
  The final triumph won
  The God of whom the prophets told
Remembrance Sunday
  O God of peace, who gave us breath
    and birth
Restoration
  Break into glad exultant song
Resurrection
  See: *Eastertide*
Return of Christ in glory
  See: *Advent*
Saints
  O God, whose throne eternal stands
  To God be glory, love and praise
  To Joseph of Nazareth God gave
    integrity
  What sense of need led Andrew on

Scripture
  See: *Bible*
Shepherd
  See: *Christ the Shepherd*
Social concern and the world's need
  Almighty Father, God of grace
  As Jesus taught us, first we pray
  Beyond what mind can measure
  Hallow the Father's Name
  O Spirit of the Sovereign Lord
  To God Most High be given
Thanksgiving
  Almighty Father, God of grace
  At the throne of grace
  Give thanks to God above
  To God Most High be given
Trinity
  Almighty Father, God of grace
  Christ pours his grace upon his own
  Glory to God, and praise
  Hallow the Father's Name
  O God of peace, who gave us breath
    and birth
  O God, whose throne eternal stands
  To God Most High be given
Trust in God
  A righteous God in heaven reigns
  Break into glad exultant song
  Give thanks to God above
  How dark the night of cloud and cares
  O God, from age to age the same
  The God of whom the prophets told
  Through stormy cloud and darkness
    deep
Unity
  Almighty Father, God of grace
  Christ pours his grace upon his own
Work
  Glory to God, and praise
  To Joseph of Nazareth God gave
    integrity
World
  See: *Peace of the world; Social concern and
    the world's need*
Worship
  See: *Praise and worship*

Index of First Lines